"I'm Allison True." She held out her hand. "Long time no see, Sammy."

Sammy? He blinked as the shock of recognition rolled through him.

"Oh, wow!" He took her small hand in his. Little sparks skidded along his arm as soon as they touched.

Sam cleared his throat. "I thought I knew you from somewhere." His gaze roamed over her face, noting the hint of freckles across her nose and her cornflower-blue eyes. "But, man, have you changed." Total understatement.

She rolled her eyes playfully. "Good! I would hate to still look like a gangly teenager."

"Nope, you're definitely not a gangly teenager anymore." *Far, far from it.* In fact, she'd grown into a beautiful woman. Not that he was really noticing.

"Glad to hear it," she said with an impish smile that he found far too appealing for a man who'd sworn to never fall in love again.

* * *

W9-CFK-744

Books by Lissa Manley

Love Inspired

*Family to the Rescue
*Mistletoe Matchmaker
*Her Small-Town Sheriff
A Snowglobe Christmas
   "A Family's Christmas Wish"
*Hometown Fireman
  Storybook Romance

*Moonlight Cove

LISSA MANLEY

decided she wanted to be a published author at the ripe old age of twelve. After she read her first romance novel as a teenager, she quickly decided romance was her favorite genre, although she still enjoys digging into a good medical thriller now and then.

When her youngest was still in diapers, Lissa needed a break from strollers and runny noses, so she sat down and started crafting a romance and has been writing ever since. Nine years later, in 2001, she sold her first book, fulfilling her childhood dream. She feels blessed to be able to write what she loves, and intends to be writing until her fingers quit working, or she runs out of heartwarming stories to tell. She's betting the fingers will go first.

Lissa lives in the beautiful city of Portland, Oregon, with her wonderful husband, a grown daughter and college-aged son, and two bossy poodles who rule the house and get away with it. When she's not writing, she enjoys reading, crafting, bargain hunting, cooking and decorating.

Storybook Romance

Lissa Manley

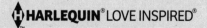

Special thanks and acknowledgment to Lissa Manley
for her participation in The Heart of Main Street series.

Recycling programs
for this product may
not exist in your area.

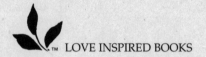 LOVE INSPIRED BOOKS

ISBN-13: 978-0-373-18947-2

STORYBOOK ROMANCE

Copyright © 2013 by Harlequin Books S.A.

www.Harlequin.com

Printed in U.S.A.

I can do all things in him who strengthens me.
—*Philippians* 4:13

This book is dedicated to my dad, Jerry.
You have been a wonderful influence in my life, and
I'm glad you needed a travel agent so many years ago.

Chapter One

"Thanks for coming in, Mr. Fibley." Allison True handed the dapper older gentleman his purchase. "I'd be glad to order more books on philately." Which was better known as stamp collecting, but Mr. Fibley, a retired pharmacist, was serious about his stamp studies and seemed to like it when Allison used the technical term for his hobby.

Thanks to the town of Bygones's Save Our Street Committee having faith in her entrepreneurial abilities, her life's dream had now come true. She was now the official owner of Happy Endings Bookstore, and she wanted to do everything possible to find, draw in and keep customers. The survival of Bygones depended on her success.

And so did her own happiness and self-respect.

Mr. Fibley's thin mouth curled into a smile. "Thank you, Miss True. I'm a dedicated philatelist, and as such, am hoping to increase my library of books on the subject." He tucked the package under his arm. "Like most of the other people in Bygones, I've been quite skeptical of the SOS Committee's plan to revitalize the town by awarding new businesses to newcomers. But I have to say, I do enjoy having a new, well-stocked bookstore here as a resource for my philately studies."

Allison returned his smile, thrilled that Mr. Fibley had changed his tune about the committee's plan. She only hoped the rest of the townspeople followed suit. Now that Randall Manufacturing had closed down, many Bygonians had been left without jobs, and many town services, such as the police force and the schools, had been put at risk. The new businesses' success was essential.

She planned on working night and day to

make sure Happy Endings stayed out of the red. After four jobs in the ten years since she'd left Bygones, she was determined not to flit away. Never mind she'd have to pay back the matching funds she'd been given to start Happy Endings if the store wasn't in the black after two years. It was do or die, and she was going to be a doer or die trying.

"Thank you, Mr. Fibley, I appreciate your support." She picked up a few of the calendar bookmarks Vivian Duncan, her one employee, had whipped up on the computer and handed them to him. "Perhaps you could hand these out to some of your friends in town and spread the word about this store, and the bakery, florist, pet store, hardware store and café, which I've listed on the back." They all had to survive to make the SOS plan work.

Bygones was hanging by a thread, and she was part of an effort to revitalize the town by starting new businesses here on Main Street while also infusing new blood into the town. Of course, she wasn't *exactly* a newcomer, but had been deemed eligible for one of the start-up, matching-fund grants provided by an anonymous benefactor because she'd been gone from town for so long. She'd be forever grateful to her sister Amy for letting her know about the SOS Committee's plans. Allison had worked all night long to get her application in on time and, thankfully, had been awarded one of the businesses.

Mr. Fibley turned his blue eyes down and perused both sides of the bookmark. "Hmm. Very clever, making this useful advertising." He drew his reading glasses out of his coat pocket and put them on, and then paused, obviously reading the text. He looked up. "Yes, I'll hand them out. In fact, my grandniece will be planning a wedding soon. I'll have her look into Sweet Dreams Bakery and Love in Bloom florist." Another small smile—just the slightest upward curve. "Definitely."

Allison glowed under his praise and was happy for his cooperation. If he could be convinced to support the newly renovated stores on Main Street, she had hope for the rest of the town. The SOS Committee had faith in her; it was good to see some of the townspeople follow suit.

Now she just needed to have faith in herself. Failing wasn't an option. Not this time.

"Wonderful. And I'm also starting creative-writing classes for teens, and have already had Story Time for the little ones several times." She glanced at her watch. "In fact, the next Story Time starts in about twenty minutes."

Mr. Fibley inclined his head. "Excellent. I'll tell my granddaughter about the Story Time program so she can bring her children."

"Thank you, Mr. Fibley, I appreciate your help, really I do." One customer at a time. Allison was determined to make this business a spectacular success. She'd given up a decent job as the manager of the Book Barn in Kansas City to come back to Bygones. And while she'd been disheartened by the big-box store's emphasis on toys and electronics, she had still walked away from her only source of income. She had invested all her savings in the funds she'd had to match to be chosen as one of the new store owners here in Bygones. Her future—everything, really—depended on making this store work.

Though it wasn't a large store by any means, it was hers, and she'd put her own stamp on the place with walls painted in soothing shades of blue, green and tan. There were comfy upholstered chairs for reading and bookshelves Allison had built herself at one of the Workshop for Women classes Gracie Wilson held at the Fixer-Upper hardware store right here on Main Street.

She still had a few bookshelves in the back room to install over in the nonfiction area, and she and Viv planned on painting some fun murals on the walls, featuring literary characters. Allison also planned on setting up a desk and computer in one corner of the store so her customers would have a place to search online for titles. In fact, the equipment was due to be delivered any day. She hoped she could figure out how to install it herself, but if not, Josh Smith, who owned the Cozy Cup Café down the street and was good with computers, would certainly help her out free. She had plenty to do and wondered how she'd get it all done. By working day and night if she had to.

Something clunked from the back of the store, drawing Allison's ever-vigilant attention. Her ears perking up, she rounded the end of the front counter and gave Mr. Fibley a wave. "Excuse me while I go see what's going on back there. Thanks again for coming in!" She glanced over and saw Viv nearby, sorting some books from a delivery that had come earlier today. Good.

Mr. Fibley waved back, a quick flick of his skinny hand in the air, and then turned to go. "I'll be back when I decide which other books I want to order."

"I'll look forward to it, Mr. Fibley," she replied as he headed out the door. "Soon you'll be able to search for titles yourself."

"Excellent," he said with another stiff wave.

Another clunk sounded, and then another. Allison decided the noise was coming from the Kids' Korner, so she picked up the pace and veered toward the back-right part of the store, creasing her brow.

She arrived in the area set up for kids, pride filling her as she noted the colorful rug and small table and chairs set up for young readers. Her gaze zeroed in on a dark-haired toddler dressed in jeans and a red shirt slowly yet methodically yanking books off a shelf, one after another. Each book fell to the floor with a heavy clunk, and in between each sound, the little guy laughed, clearly enjoying the sound of his relatively harmless yet messy play.

Allison rushed over, noting there was no adult in sight. "Hey, there, bud," she said, keeping her voice soft and nonconfrontational. "Whatcha doing?"

He turned big brown eyes fringed with long, dark eyelashes toward her. He looked vaguely familiar, even though she was certain she'd never met this little boy. Odd.

"Fun!" A chubby hand sent another book crashing to the floor. He giggled and stomped his feet on the floor in a little happy dance, clearly thrilled with his own antics. "See?"

Carefully she reached out and stilled his marauding hands. "Whoa, there, little guy." She gently pulled him away. "The books are supposed to stay on the shelf." Holding on to him, she cast her gaze about the enclosed area, but her view was limited by the tall bookshelves lined up from the edge of the Kids' Korner to the front of the store. "Are you here with your mommy or daddy?" She hadn't seen this little guy come in, but then again, she had been busy with Mr. Fibley back in the nonfiction area.

The boy tugged. "Daddy!" he squealed.

"Nicky!" a deep masculine voice replied behind her. "Oh, man. Looks like you've been making a mess."

A nebulous sense of familiarity swept through her at the sound of that voice. Not breathing, still holding the boy's hand, Allison slowly turned around. Her whole body froze and her heart gave a little spasm, then fell to her toes as she looked into deep brown eyes that matched Nicky's.

Sam Franklin. The only man Allison had ever loved.

Sam tightened his hold on Rosalie and stared at the slender, pretty brunette holding Nicky's hand. She stared back at him, her gorgeous blue eyes wide, her glossy pink lips slack. Something about her rang a distant bell, but…why?

Rosalie squawked and squirmed in his arms, yanking his thoughts away from the attractive young woman obviously trying to keep control of Nicky. "Daddy! Put me down!" Rosie commanded.

"I've got this one," the blue-eyed gal said.

"Thanks." Sam's parenting persona clicked into action. "What's the special word, Rosie?"

"Pleeeze?" Rosie squeaked, still squirming.

"All right, here you go," he said, setting her on the floor, straightening the pink-and-white-striped top she wore. Pink was her favorite color, followed a close second by purple. Or *poiple,* as Rosie said.

Rosie ran over and held a finger up in front of her brother's face. "No, no, Nicky!"

Nicky scowled. "Don't boss me, Ro-ro!"

Sam shook his head, amused by the push-pull dynamic between the twins, though he was sure his amusement would fade by the time he wrestled them into bed tonight. He loved them more than anything, but they ex-hausted him. Being a single parent wasn't easy, although his ex-wife had certainly seemed to sail through handling the twins when she'd had them. Of course, her new fiancé, Spense O'Laughlin, was there to help. That thought sent a dart of bitterness through Sam, which he did his best to ignore.

The brunette raised her brows. "Oh, she's quite the bossy one, isn't she?"

Sam stepped forward, noticing how the young woman's pink sweater set off her blue eyes just right, and gently took a hold of Rosie's rigid finger. "She was born bossy."

Nicky tried to dart away, but his pretty captor held him tight. "And he's the mischievous one, right?"

Sam plucked Nicky up with his free arm. "Right," he said, impressed by her kid-corralling skills. "Rosie here bosses, and he causes trouble."

"You've got your hands full, then," she said with a quirk of her lips, putting her hands into the front pockets of her well-fitting jeans.

He hiked Nicky up farther as the little boy squirmed. "You could say that. Twins are very challenging." Understatement. Never mind that he never felt he had a very good handle on the single-dad thing.

Big blue eyes regarded him for a long moment, and again that sense of familiarity misted through Sam. Where had he seen her before? Unease had him shifting from foot to foot.

Rosie pointed at Sam's rescuer and piped in with, "I want to see that necklace." The woman gave Rosie an indulgent smile and squatted until she was at Rosie's level. "See?" she said, holding out the chunky gold chain around her neck.

Rosie fingered it. "It's pretty!"

"Thank you," the woman said. Then after a few moments, she looked up and said, "You don't recognize me, do you, Sam?"

His face heated. Yeah. She obviously recognized him, but he had no idea who she was. Awkward. "Um…no, I don't," he answered honestly. "But you do look familiar."

She lifted the necklace over her head and handed it to Rosie.

Rosie crowed in delight.

The gal rose and stepped forward. "I'm Allison True, your sister Lori's best friend from growing up?" She held out her hand. "Long time, no see, Sammy."

Sammy? He blinked as shock rolled through him, and he froze for a second, staring at her. Suddenly, everything meshed and recognition clicked into place. "Oh, wow!" He took her small hand in his. Little sparks skidded along his arm as soon as they touched.

"Surprise!" Allison smiled, exposing straight white teeth devoid of the braces she'd worn in high school. "It's me."

He cleared his throat and reclaimed his hand. "I knew I knew you from somewhere, but I couldn't place you." He roamed his gaze over her face, noting her smooth, creamy complexion, with just a hint of freckles across her nose. She had a delicate jawline and cornflower-blue eyes, which he now recalled were called the True-blue eyes because everybody in the True family had them. "But, man, have you changed." Another understatement. He remembered her mostly as a nerdy bookworm who wore glasses and her hair in braids, though she had blossomed in high school and he'd actually wanted to ask her out.

She rolled her eyes playfully. "Good thing. I would hate to look like the gangly teenager I was the last time I saw you." She made a face. "Ugh."

He nodded. "Nope, you're definitely not a gangly teenager anymore." Far, far from it. In fact, she'd grown into a beautiful woman. Not that he was really noticing.... All right, he was, but only in a very observational kind of way. As in, hey, she'd changed a lot.

"Glad to hear it," she said with an impish smile that he found very appealing.

Nicky kicked his legs. "Put me down, Daddy!"

"Let's stay up here, dude," Sam replied. "We need to leave the bookstore standing."

"Nooo!" Nicky cried. "I want down!"

Allison stepped forward. "Hey, Nicky. What's your favorite thing in the whole world?"

"Cars," Nicky replied, pushing at Sam's shoulders. It was hard to contain this busy little boy for long. On the other hand, Rosie had plopped herself down on the floor to play with the necklace Allison had given her to look at. How could two siblings be so different?

"Cars?" Allison cocked her head to the side. "Well, I know where we can find some books about cars."

Nicky stilled and turned to Allison. "You do?"

"Sure," Allison said. "Would you like to see?"

"Yes!" Nicky replied.

"What's the special word?" Sam automatically asked as he put Nicky down.

"Please?" Nicky responded.

Sam looked at Allison. "You sure you don't mind?"

"Of course not. This is a bookstore, a place to look at books." She held out a hand to Nicky. "Right, Nicky?"

He took her hand. "Right!" he said, jumping in place.

"Well, right this way," Allison said with a tug on Nicky's hand.

"Can I come, too?" Rosie said.

Allison held out her other hand. "Of course. What kind of books do you like?"

Rosie took her hand. "Princess books," she replied with a jump of her own.

"Okay, we have those," Allison said with an indulgent smile.

Sam shook his head. Boy, she really had a way with them.

Allison led them to a kid-size table and chairs set in the corner. "Why don't you two sit down here at the table and I'll get you the books you want, all right?"

Both three-year-olds immediately sat down. "'Kay," they said in unison.

"We'll stay here," Rosie said.

"Yeah, right here," Nicky added, patting the table with his chubby little hands.

Sam's jaw fell. He could never get the twins to do much of anything at the same time, much less sit still. One of the many challenges of parenting twins. It didn't help that his former wife, Teresa, was always criticizing everything he did. "Wow, you've really got the touch," he said to Allison.

She smiled and waggled her eyebrows, then

gestured at the shelves surrounding them. "No, I've just got the books."

"Well, whatever you've got, it's working." Sam rubbed his jaw. "Maybe I need some pointers."

"Ask away," Allison said as she went to a shelf on the left side. She pulled down a large book. "I'm somewhat of an expert on kids."

He drew his eyebrows together. "Do you have kids?" He forced himself not to look at her left ring finger.

"No, I'm not married, so no kids. But, if you remember, I took care of my younger sisters all the time when we were growing up, so I've got some experience." She set the book on the table in front of Nicky.

"That's right. You had, what, three younger siblings?"

"Just two," she said, holding up two fingers as she went to a different shelf. "Amanda and Amy."

"I remember now. You were the oldest, and Lori often went to your house because you had to babysit all the time." More details came back to him. "Your parents owned the wheat spread on the outskirts of town, right?"

She pulled another book from the shelf. "Yup, and they still do." She shrugged stiffly. "Although I don't babysit for them anymore."

He noticed her rigid shoulders and wondered what they signified but didn't want to pry. Instead, he said, "Your sisters are still in high school, right?" He'd seen them around the school, but he hadn't had either of them in class yet.

"Right. Amanda works at Sweet Dreams Bakery."

More details materialized. "I seem to remember Lori telling me you moved away some time ago, correct?"

Allison set the book in front of Rosie. "Here you go, sweet pea."

The endearment made his throat tight.

Allison looked up at Sam. "That's right. I had a job opportunity in Kansas City after I graduated from high school, and I lived there until just a few months ago when I was selected by the SOS Committee to run this store."

"You always were a book lover, weren't you?" Another memory surfaced. "In fact, didn't you and Lori start your own book club way back when?"

Allison's big blue eyes went round. "You remember that?"

"I do."

She smiled. "Good memory. Yes, I've always loved books."

"You must be thrilled to have this store, then."

She sat down next to Nicky. "Definitely. This is my dream come true, honestly. I have to make this place work."

"Yeah, a lot's riding on the SOS plan panning out." Such as his job as a math teacher at the high school. If the plan didn't right the economy in Bygones, the schools and the police force would be the first to go. In fact, Sam had already put out feelers for teaching jobs elsewhere in case the SOS plan didn't work. Although with Teresa threatening to try to get sole custody, his future was up in the air in a lot of ways.

"I work at the high school, and my job is at

risk," he confided. They'd managed to keep the school district going since Randall Manufacturing had closed, but how much longer would funds hold out? He hoped the SOS Committee's plan to revitalize the town with the six new stores on this block would pan out. Then his job would be safe, and he could focus on the kids.

"Yes, I realize that." Her eyes shone with determination. "But all the other new shop owners are just as determined as I am to make this block a success."

He shook his head. "I'm sure you all have good intentions, but I have my doubts about the SOS plan. A lot of people have already moved away, and despite the anonymous benefactor's generosity, the town is still floundering."

"Hopefully that will all change."

"Well, I'm not counting on anything," he said. "I've already put out feelers for other jobs."

"Oh, no. You're planning on moving away?"

He set his jaw. "Hopefully not. But I need a

job, and I might not have one here. I have to be practical." His life was a mess right now.

"Yes, I suppose so." She gave him a look rife with speculation. "Who do you think the benefactor is?"

"No idea," he said. "Whoever it is has taken great pains to stay anonymous."

She opened her mouth to reply, then froze. "Oh!" Glancing quickly at her watch, she sprang to her feet. "It's almost time for Story Time."

"Story Time?" he repeated.

"I want to go to Story Time," Rosie announced. "Please, Daddy?"

"Me, too," Nicky said. "I like stories." He stood, his small hands struggling to pick up the big car book Allison had brought him. "Lots."

Allison grinned and her nose crinkled in the most appealing way. "I'm sure they'd love it." She came closer.

The scent of peaches floated to him. He once again noticed the barest hint of freckles sprinkling her pert nose and he had to smother the urge to count every one. Words stuck in his throat. Whoa. He hadn't ever had the urge to count anyone's freckles…

"Whaddya say?" Allison leaned in. More peaches.

He fought the urge to inhale deeply.

At that moment, Nicky took off, shouting, "Story Time! Let's go!"

Allison went after him, looking back, her eyes alight with excitement. "If you stay, you might get a few minutes of peace and quiet," she said. "I'll round him up."

Sam cleared his throat, liking her can-do attitude. "Oh, well, sure, we'll stay. Thanks." Anything to keep the kids occupied, Nicky in particular. Though watching Allison wouldn't be a chore on Sam's part— Oh, man! Where had that thought come from?

She gave him a thumbs-up. "Great." She disappeared around the corner bookshelf, hot on Nicky's heels, taking her appealing peach scent with her.

Sam started breathing again.

Rosie, ever the calm little lady, sedately carried her book over and stood next to Sam. "I like her," she said, her chubby cheeks creased with a smile. "She's nice."

He put his hand on Rosie's dark hair. "I do, too, sweetie." In another life he'd probably ask her out.

Rosie took his hand and tugged on it. "Come on, Daddy. Let's go to Story Time!"

He let himself be led by his daughter, taking a moment to corral his thoughts, reminding himself that he wasn't looking for any kind of romantic relationship. Teresa had cheated on him and left him for Spense. That was bad enough. Terrible, actually. But worse yet, she'd been making noises about going for full custody. At this point, fresh off a traumatic divorce, Sam was leery of romance and had, on the advice of his lawyer, chosen not to risk custody issues with any kind of dating at the moment. Nothing was worth losing his kids.

Right now his life was about his job and Nicky and Rosie. There wasn't room for anything more. That was just the way it was, and he didn't have the time or energy to fight the truth, much less the stomach for constant conflict with Teresa. What else could a good father do?

The story rug was right around the bookcase, tucked into the far corner of the store. Allison already had Nicky sitting on the round, fluffy, bright red rug alongside three other kids who looked to be about the twins' age. Sam spied Allison at a bookshelf to the left, searching for a title.

Women who were obviously the moms of the kids sat in adult-size chairs lined up at the outer rim of the rug. Sam led Rosie to the rug, and then retreated to the background, wanting a bird's-eye view of Nicky since he rarely sat still for much of anything. The kiddo had two speeds—off and way, way on—so Sam wanted to be prepared to herd him back to the rug when Nicky popped up, on to whatever caught his fickle attention.

Allison settled herself into an upholstered chair facing the kids, a book in her hands, her face glowing, her mouth formed into a brilliant smile that had his breath hitching again in a very alarming way. Even so, he felt himself automatically honing in on her pretty face, her big, expressive eyes in particular.

"Okay, story listeners, can we all quiet down, please?" She paused, her brows raised, clearly waiting for the kids to focus in on her.

After a few moments all five kids quieted and turned their attention to her. "Excellent work at listening," she said, giving a gentle nod to each child in turn. "So. Are you all ready for a really fun story about a steam shovel?"

An excited chorus rose from the children. "Yes!"

Nicky stood up. "I love steam shovels!" he crowed, his hands in the air.

"I do, too," Allison replied with a patient smile. "But we all have to sit crisscross applesauce on the story rug before the story can begin."

Rosie tugged on Nicky's arm. "Sit down, Nicky." She pointed to her crisscross position on the floor. "See?"

Sam held his breath, hoping Nicky went against tradition and sat down, preparing himself to swoop in and take control if necessary.

Nicky jerked his arm away from his sister, defiance clear in the tilt of his chin. "Don't boss me, Ro-Ro."

Uh-oh. Typical conflict between the twins: Rosie trying to boss Nicky and Nicky rebelling. Sam prepared to head their way to break up the skirmish.

Allison piped in, her voice calm and soothing. "Nicky, I forgot to say that every story listener who sits quietly will get to come up here and help me turn the pages."

Nicky's head swung her way. "Me, too?"

"If you sit quietly, yes." She pointed to the spot on the rug next to Rosie. "So, would you please sit down crisscross applesauce, and we'll start the story about the steam shovel?"

Sam braced for a meltdown; it could go either way with Nicky. He was a good kid, but not as mature as Rosie, and didn't always deal well with following directions, especially if they went against what he wanted to do. Pair that with his headstrong personality and the end result was often a messy fit that could be heard three blocks away.

"Can I help first?" Nicky asked.

Sam cringed as his son's impatient side made an appearance. He sneaked a glance at the other moms, embarrassed, but they seemed to be taking the holdup in stride. In fact, one was texting on her cell phone and wasn't paying any attention at all.

"Whoever sits still and is quietest gets to help first," Allison said.

Nicky instantly plopped down. "I'll sit." He rested his chin on his knees.

Allison gave Nicky an approving smile. "Good choice, Nicky." She held up the book, facing outward, and turned to the first page. "Let's begin."

She proceeded to read the story about Mike Mulligan and his steam shovel, Mary Anne. Sam had heard the story when he was a kid, so he was familiar with the plot, and how Mike and Mary Anne went to the country and dug the town hall basement in a day but didn't leave themselves a ramp to get out.

Even though the story wasn't new to him,

he listened, transfixed, as Allison made the story come alive using uniquely creative voices for each of the characters. She read at just the right pace and knew how to point out relevant things in the illustrations as she narrated the story. She truly had a gift for storytelling.

All the kids listened intently, including Nicky. Partway through the book, Allison invited Nicky and a little blonde girl with curly hair to help her turn the pages. Nicky jumped up, grinning, and stood still at Allison's side and took turns turning the pages with the little girl.

Amazed, Sam watched Nicky follow directions and share responsibility. Willingly. With his heart getting mushy, Sam let his gaze drift to Allison. She had a way with kids, no doubt about it. *His* kid in particular. She knew exactly how to handle Nicky. He only wished he could be half as patient and able as she was. Guilt shot through him and struck a familiar blow to his conscience; the divorce had been hardest on the kids.

Relaxing for a few precious moments, he

let his gaze wander to Nicky and Rosie, then over to Allison. Inevitably, he thought back to his senior year in high school, when Allison had started to bloom and he'd started noticing her as more than just a friend. She may have considered herself a "gangly teenager," but Sam now recalled when that had all started to change.

Lori had discouraged him from dating Allison, afraid it would cost them their friendship if a relationship between him and Allison didn't work out. Besides, Lori had asked, would he remain committed to her after he went off to college? He hadn't been sure—what eighteen-year-old guy would be?—so he'd dropped the idea, not ready to settle down. He'd gone off to college, and that had been that.

He looked at Allison now, noting her patience, kindness, ready smile and fresh, understated beauty.

And couldn't help but wonder if he hadn't made a big mistake ten years ago.

Chapter Two

A whisper from behind Sam interrupted the tough questions running through his head. "It's good to see her back in Bygones, isn't it?"

He turned. Mrs. Coraline Connolly, the principal at Bygones High School and his boss, stood there, dressed in blue pants and a red sweater with big gold buttons on the front. Her short gray hair was styled perfectly as always, and her blue eyes sparkled with intelligence behind her wire-rimmed glasses. She was petite, but no pushover, and not a woman to be underestimated.

"Yes, it is," he answered in a whisper, rising. He pointed toward the front of the store to indicate they should move so they didn't interrupt Story Time with their conversation.

Coraline got the gist and spryly headed away from the Kids' Korner. Sam followed.

She turned, smiling, when she reached a far aisle closer to the front of the store. "Looks as if your twins are enjoying Story Time."

"Yes, they are. Allison is a great story-teller."

"She certainly is. I can't think of a better person to run this store." Coraline eyed him speculatively. "I seem to remember your sister was quite close to her while growing up." Before she was principal of Bygones High School, Coraline had been a teacher, so she knew everyone who'd grown up here better than just about anybody else in town.

"Uh-huh. Allison and I were just talking about that."

Coraline smiled. "Is this the first time you've been into Happy Endings?"

"I'm sorry to say it is. I wish I'd brought the kids in sooner." Especially now that he'd seen how well Allison handled them. "Story Time might become a regular thing."

"Did you know Allison was running the store?" asked Coraline, shifting her purse from one arm to the other.

"No," he said sheepishly. "I've been pretty busy with teaching, after-school tutoring and coaching."

"And your darling twins, of course," Coraline said with a lift of a brow. "I'm sure they take up most of your spare time."

"Well, that goes without saying." On the nights he had the kids, he stayed up late grading papers after putting them to bed, then fell into an exhausted sleep himself. And when he didn't have the kids, he still had catch-up classroom work to do in the evenings, along with early mornings. Whether the twins were with him or not, he always seemed to be running on empty.

"You probably don't get out much, do you?" Coraline, a widow, had raised four children, so she knew what it was like to be a busy working parent.

"No, I don't."

"You need some time with other adults."

"Yeah, I guess my social life could use

some work." Frankly, though, dealing with the ups and downs of social relationships was just more than he could handle right now.

"Have you thought about spending some time with any of the wonderful young women here in town?" she asked in her usual no-nonsense way.

Which was her way of asking if he was ready to date. He shook his head, wishing he hadn't admitted his social life was dead. "No, I'm not ready for that yet. Besides, when I have the twins with me, I don't feel right about leaving them." True enough. He only had them half the time, so he tried to spend as much time with them as possible.

"Of course not," Coraline replied. "It's been, what? A year since your split with Teresa?"

"Fourteen months, actually."

"That long?" Coraline blinked. "My, how time flies."

"It certainly does." Though why did it seem as if he'd been by himself forever? And would be for the foreseeable future. So be it.

She patted his arm. "Well, I'm sure you'll

come around and want to revive your social life soon." Her gaze strayed in the direction of the Kids' Korner. "Allison is single, isn't she?"

He was suddenly on high alert; Coraline was known for her matchmaking tendencies. "Um…yes, I believe she is."

"And she's good with your children?"

"Seems to be," he replied neutrally. How could he get Coraline off the track she'd taken?

"She's a very nice young woman," Coraline said, her voice going up just enough to remind him she was probably fishing.

"Yes, she is." Pretty, too, though he was determined not to get caught up in that detail. Teresa was gorgeous, and look how that had turned out.

Coraline sighed. "I'm just going to be direct. Do you have any interest in dating Allison?"

He wasn't surprised by the question. He was an eligible single man. "Coraline, while I know you have my best interests at heart, I'm not interested in dating Allison, or anyone else, for that matter." Coraline had good intentions, so he'd be polite.

She frowned and her eyes went soft. "Your divorce wounded you, didn't it?"

Put mildly. "Yes, it did." He wasn't a liar, and even if he were, an untruth wouldn't slip by a sharp gal like Coraline. "Especially because of the way the whole thing played out." It was common knowledge that Teresa had left him for Spense O'Laughlin, an up-and-coming lawyer who'd moved to Bygones a few years ago to take over a law practice in nearby Manhattan, Kansas, from his uncle.

"Ah, yes, I'm sure that made the whole thing worse," Coraline said, her voice tinged with sympathy.

"That would be an understatement." Their marriage had been on the rocks for a while— Teresa, a city girl, hated living in Bygones, and blamed Sam for keeping them there— but Sam had been willing to tough it out and stay together for the kids' sakes.

Until the horrible night Teresa told him she'd fallen in love with Spense and was leaving Sam. Sam's heart had shriveled up on the spot, and he'd known then that there was no saving the marriage, especially when he'd found out that Spense had told Teresa they could move to Kansas City as soon as he could sell his practice. The proverbial final nail in the coffin had been hammered home.

There had been no happy ending for Sam, just as there'd been no happy ending for his dad, who'd never been the same since Sam's mom had left him to go "find herself" in a commune in Colorado when Sam was eleven.

Given that, Sam was sure such a thing as a happy ending didn't even exist, except in the books sold by the store in which he stood.

"Divorce is never easy." Coraline thought for a moment. "Your guard is up now, isn't it?"

"Pretty much," he replied. "The last thing I want is another heartbreak." He'd had enough of that, considering his and Teresa's history, coupled with his mom's desertion. In hind-sight, he shouldn't have gotten married in the first place, because he and Teresa were such different people. But love and attraction had skewed his judgment—lesson learned. And while there was undeniably bitterness in his heart due to Teresa's betrayal, his marriage had produced his precious children, and he would always be thankful for that immense blessing.

"Another love might be different," Coraline said with a knowing look. "And you're still a young man—too young to be alone for the rest of your life."

"Perhaps," he said, though his response wasn't accurate; the past didn't lie. But he respected Coraline too much to go with the truth and denounce her statement outright.

"I'll pray for you about this, all right?" Coraline was a pillar of Bygones Community Church and had an abiding faith Sam marveled at and envied.

"That would be wonderful," he replied, not wanting to offend Coraline, appreciating her sentiment, though he had heavy doubts prayer would work. Hadn't his been left unanswered?

Her eyes slipped past him. "Oh, looks like Story Time is over. Here comes your darling son."

"Daddy!" Nicky cried, grabbing Sam by the knees. "I just heard a story about Mike and Mary Anne!"

Sam turned and scooped Nicky up into his arms. "I know you did, bud."

Coraline held out her hand for a high five. "And what a good listener you were."

Nicky tapped her palm with his chubby one. "I got to turn pages!"

"Excellent," Coraline replied with a gentle smile. "You did a great job."

Sam looked down at Nicky. "What do you say?"

"Thank you!" Nicky exclaimed.

"You're very welcome." Coraline moved her purse to her other arm again, her direct gaze zeroing in on Sam. "You'll think about what I said?"

He inclined his head left, nodding. "Of course." Another platitude for a worthy cause and a good-hearted woman. He'd hardened his heart quite a while ago and intended to keep it that way.

"Good. Now I'm off to pick out a book on organic gardening." With a wave, she turned and headed farther into the store, moving with a spring in her step Sam could only hope he would have at her age.

Nicky chattered on and on about the story as Sam went back to the Kids' Korner in search of Rosie.

He found her on the floor in the middle of the story rug, "reading" a book. Allison knelt next to her, her finger pointing out something on the current page. Rosie turned and smiled at Allison, and Allison ever so gently smoothed one of Rosie's dark curls back off her face. Rosie giggled, and then mimicked Allison and smoothed a stray lock of burnished hair back from Allison's face, then patted her cheek. The look of adoration on his daughter's face was plain to see.

Sam stared, unable to look away from the touching picture the two of them made sitting there, two brunettes, a girl and a woman with no connection except for the one formed today.

And for just a moment he wished that the past hadn't shadowed the present with such profound lessons and that he didn't have to keep such a tight rein on his heart.

Allison looked up from her spot on the floor with Rosie and saw Sam standing there with Nicky in his arms. Sam looked very much the athlete-coach in his high-end black athletic sweats and black-and-white basketball shoes. His short dark hair was attractively mussed and he was slightly tanned, as if he spent time outside on the weekends.

The sight of him had always made her knees shaky, but seeing him now, as a loving, devoted dad, made every cell in her body quake. Add that to how mushy her heart felt from Rosie's gentle face pats and Nicky's wide-eyed fascination with Mike and Mary Anne, and Allison felt downright giddy. She loved kids.

But Sam? She'd heard he was in town and had avoided him. She just hadn't been ready to face him.

But…now she had faced him, and she'd survived just fine. And in the here and now she could be giddy over his adorable kids.

No harm there. In fact, that could only lead to good things all around.

That thought put a genuine smile on her face as she rose and held out her hand for Rosie. "Would you like to sit at the table and look at that book?"

Rosie took Allison's hand and clambered up from the floor, somehow bringing the book with her. "Okay." She looked at Nicky as she headed to the kids' table and chairs Allison had set up. "Nicky, bring a car book over here and sit with me. We can read!"

"Daddy, put me down," Nicky commanded. "I'm gonna read with Rosie." He paused. "Please?"

As Sam obeyed Nicky's request, Allison grabbed another car book from the shelf. "How about this one, Nicky? It looks like it has some pretty good pictures of cars in it."

Nicky ran over. "Yeah! Lots of cars," he said, taking the book from her.

Sam followed him to stand beside Allison. "Kids, we can stay for a few more minutes, but I have to get to practice very soon."

The twins settled themselves at the table. "Okay," they said in unison.

Allison smiled. "They're being very cooperative."

"For now," Sam said. "Guess I better enjoy it."

"Sounds as if they're quite a handful."

"What three-year-old isn't?"

"True." Allison looked at the twins, who were obviously two bundles of energy. "And you've got double the handful, right?"

"Yes, but only half the time."

"So you share custody?" she asked, curious about his situation. Who wouldn't be?

He nodded. "Yeah."

"How's that going?"

"All right, but I miss them like crazy when they're with Teresa."

"That has to be rough," Allison said. If she ever had kids—which she hoped to someday, in the future, after she had her career cemented in stone—she couldn't imagine not having them with her full-time. And she definitely hadn't inherited her parents' workaholic tendencies; she believed in actually spending time with one's children.

"Yep. The house just seems too quiet, you know?" He looked at his watch. "Oh, man, we've got to run. I still have to drop the kids at Teresa's before I head to practice."

Teresa. His ex-wife. Allison had seen her once at the Hometown Grocery store but hadn't ever spoken to her. She was tall and blonde and very pretty in a classic Southern-belle way. Teresa had left Sam for another man. News like that traveled at lightning speed in a small town like Bygones. Allison wouldn't dream of bringing it up.

"How's the team this year?" she asked. Both her sisters played basketball for Bygones High School, so she was interested.

He made a wiggly motion in the air with his hand. "Not bad. One kid in particular is particularly promising, but his academic struggles might keep him from playing."

"Well, if he has reading and writing problems, he might be interested in the creative-writing workshops I'm starting here next week."

Sam raised his eyebrows. "I hadn't heard about that."

"Coraline Connolly and I came up with the idea as a way to bring in business and serve the community at the same time." She pointed toward the front of the store. "I'll go get you a flyer while you round up the kids."

"Great," he replied. "I can't guarantee Rory will be interested, but I'll pass the info along just the same."

"I'd appreciate it." A thought occurred to her. "And if you want to dangle a carrot, let Rory know that there are several high school girls already signed up for the workshop, including my youngest sister, Amy."

Sam grinned. "That ought to do the trick. If there's anything that will motivate a teenage boy it's the chance to be around a teenage girl."

How she wished that had been true for Sam in regards to her way back when; obviously he'd never seen her in that light, no matter how hard she'd wished it to be true. She wouldn't be making that misguided mistake again. "I say use any ammunition at our disposal."

"I agree." He gave her a pointed look. "I have to say, I really admire how hard you're working to make this place a success."

A rosy glow spread through her, warming her from the inside out. "Well, thanks. I want it to be a success for me, but also for the town." She pressed her lips together. "A lot of people don't think the SOS Committee's plan will work, and I want to prove them wrong." She also wanted to prove it to her parents, who'd been livid when she'd told them she was leaving for Kansas City. They'd assumed she'd stay in Bygones and continue to provide live-in babysitting for her sisters in their absence. They'd made it clear they thought she'd fail when she left, and their doubts had crept into her and taken root. They'd said the same thing when she'd returned to run Happy Endings, and she'd feared they were right. Especially since one job in Kansas City had turned into a succession of four that had never been a good fit. Self-fulfilling prophecy laid down by her parents' misgivings? Maybe.

Well, she was done with trying to escape her problems by moving on, hoping to find the pie in the sky that would make her happy. She'd returned to Bygones and staked all her financial and emotional resources on Happy Endings. That, along with the faith the SOS Committee had put in her, had solidified her determination to make Happy Endings a success. Hearing praise from Sam simply confirmed all this.

"Seems you have a bit of a stubborn streak," he replied. "That's a good thing in my book."

More glowing warmed her. "I hope so. Sometimes my stubbornness gets me into trouble." Such as when she'd stubbornly— and foolishly—held on to her adoration for Sam in high school, though he'd never expressed one iota of interest in her. It was time for her to use her stubbornness toward more concrete goals.

Nicky ran up. "Daddy, read with me."

Sam touched Nicky on the head. "We gotta get going, bud."

"No!" Nicky said, running back over to his book. "I wanna stay." He gave Sam a defiant stare, full of three-year-old bravado.

Seeing a conflict on the horizon, Allison piped in, "Would you like to come back to another Story Time?"

Rosie jumped up. "Yes. I do."

"Me, too," Nicky called out. "When?"

"Well," Allison said with a conspiratorial look at Sam, "we have Story Time every Monday and Wednesday afternoon at four o'clock. Today is Monday, so we will have another one day after tomorrow. Will you two come?" She gave Sam a teasing look. "You can come, too, if you want."

"Oh, is that so?" he said with a glint in his eyes that made Allison's tummy drop. "You don't think they should come by themselves?"

Nicky and Rosie rushed over in unison, precluding Allison's response. "Please, can we, Daddy? Please?" they begged in an excited tangle of words, each hopping around Sam like little monkeys.

Sam laughed. "Okay, okay. We'll come

back on Wednesday, but only if you two co-operate now so I can get to practice."

Rosie glared at Nicky. "You cooperate, Nicky." She grabbed his arm. "Daddy says."

Nicky jerked his arm loose. "Don't boss me, Ro-ro," he said, his eyebrows scrunched together. Then he paused and regarded Sam. "I o'operate with you, Daddy."

"Thank you," Sam replied, with a gentle rub to Nicky's dark hair. "Dad likes it when you do that."

Allison liked everything about this little family. Not that she'd ever be part of it. But she would look forward to seeing the twins every once in a while. Sam, too, but only as an old friend. Nothing more than that.

The four of them walked to the front of the store. Allison grabbed some workshop flyers and gave them to Sam.

He took them, promising to give one to Rory and some of the other basketball-team members, too.

Allison lingered by Sam's side as they all made their way toward the door, loath to see them go. She couldn't remember when she'd enjoyed a Story Time more; sharing her love of books with others was gratifying.

"What do you say to Allison?" he asked the twins when they reached the double doors leading out to Main Street.

"Thank you!" the two darlings said in unison.

"You're very welcome," Allison replied. "I'll be sure and pick out really neat stories for you two at the next Story Time, all right?"

"Yay!" they crowed, again together.

"I owe you a big thank-you, too," Sam said, his chocolate-brown eyes shining with sincerity. "These two don't usually settle down much, so it was a nice break for me to have them interested in something else."

"Books are a great way to keep kids occupied," she replied dutifully.

"I think it was the storyteller who kept them enthralled." He squeezed her upper arm. "Kudos to you."

His praise, as well as his touch, had her lighting up like a sparkler again. "I love exposing kids to literature, so it was not a chore, trust me."

"We'll count on seeing you on Wednesday."

She'd also look forward to it. Because of the kids, of course.

Sam opened the door and he and the twins left. When they reached the curb, he turned and waved, his dark hair shining like polished walnuts in the early-autumn sun, his teeth flashing in a smile that almost stopped Allison's heart.

She stood there for a few moments, unable to drag her gaze away. Sam took a twin's hand in each of his and walked across the street and her heart twisted. What adorable children—a handful, yes, but that was to be expected at their age. And to think they might have been hers if her dreams of marrying Sam and having his babies had come true.

But that's just what they were—girlish dreams, not reality. She was older now, and wiser. Of course, she had to keep up her guard; her focus now was her business, not romance.

But the twins… Well, she had no idea how she would manage to stay away from them.

Chapter Three

Allison made herself turn from the window, only to come up against Coraline Connolly's bright blue gaze. "Oh, hi, Coraline. I didn't see you come in." She noted the large book in the older woman's arms. "Did you find everything you need?"

Coraline bestowed a beatific smile on Allison. "Oh, yes, I discovered quite a lot here today."

Was Coraline referring to more than reading material? Allison drew her eyebrows together. "Um…okay. Excellent." She headed to the check-out counter. "It looks like you located the book you wanted."

"Oh, yes, dear, I did." She held up the book.

"I want to try my hand at organic gardening next spring, so I'm going to purchase this book."

"Excellent!" Since Viv was helping another customer at register one, Allison stopped at register two. "Anything else today?"

"Yes. I wanted to ask how things are going with you and Mayor Langston." The mayor was Allison's main contact, and host of sorts, from the SOS Committee. He owned the Hometown Grocery, which was run by his wife, Helen, and he was somewhat of a bookworm himself, which was why he had been assigned to be her host. Allison guessed he was in his mid- to late-fifties.

"Oh, things are going really well with him. In fact, he just stopped by yesterday afternoon, and he was very pleased with the plans you and I have made for the creative-writing workshops."

"Perfect. Glad to hear that's all working out." Coraline put the book on the counter. "There's something else I wanted to discuss with you."

"Yes?" As a founding member of the SOS

Committee and a longtime resident of Bygones, Coraline had a vested interest in ensuring the committee's plan was successful.

Coraline leaned in. "I just wanted to know if you're still in love with Sam Franklin."

Allison felt her jaw go so slack she was surprised it wasn't resting on the counter. "Wh-what?" She hadn't told anybody she'd loved Sam, not even Lori.

"Are you still in love with Sam?" Coraline repeated.

The change of subject had thrown Allison, but she recovered in a moment. "No," she managed to say in all truthfulness. She'd put those feelings behind long ago, and that's where they would stay.

Coraline peered at her. "But you were in love with him in high school, right?"

Lying wasn't an option, so Allison said, "Yes, I was. But that was ages ago." She fiddled with a bag. "How did you know?"

"Oh, it was as obvious as the nose on my face." Coraline turned her lips up into a small smile. "I guess you could say I have a nose for these kinds of things." She chuckled.

"Wow." Allison shook her head. "I thought I was pretty good at hiding my feelings."

"Oh, you were. But when you changed your schedule every year to be in the same classes as Sam, I had an inkling there might be a pretty strong crush going on."

Allison's face warmed. "I thought I was being so clever."

"You were. I'm just cleverer…and I did the same thing in college years ago when I wanted to be in the same classes as my dearly departed Jasper."

"Ah. That explains it." Allison picked up the book. "I'm relieved to know my feelings weren't common knowledge."

"I'm assuming Sam never knew?" Coraline asked.

Allison scanned the bar code on the gardening book. "No way. I would have been mortified if he had found out."

"Because he didn't feel the same way?"

"Right." Allison had just been his sister's pesky, nerdy friend, not dating material as far as Sam was concerned. She'd never felt worthy of him. "He was always dating someone prettier, more outgoing. I didn't stand a chance."

"Unrequited love is tricky, isn't it?" Coraline pulled her wallet out of her purse. "Kind of an odd mix of wanting the other person to know and, well, not."

"Exactly, especially when you're a gawky teenage girl with no self-confidence." Allison looked at the total. "That'll be seventeen ninety-nine."

Coraline handed Allison a twenty. "I always suspected you left town because of heartbreak."

Allison blinked. Was there no end to Coraline's dead-on observations? She had an uncanny eye for details, and a taste for matchmaking, it seemed. "Partly." Allison made change as she went on. "I was devastated when he left town for college." She handed the money to Coraline. "The other part involved a job at a large bookstore in Kansas City." And escaping her parents. But she wouldn't say that.

"But now you're back, and Sam is single."

Coraline tucked her wallet back into her purse. "Maybe a second chance is possible?"

"No, it's not," Allison replied quickly and firmly.

"After all he went through with his wife's betrayal, Sam needs a good Christian woman, and so do those darling twins of his."

Unexpected longing spread through Allison like a burst dam, but she recovered quickly and set those feelings aside. What else could she do? "I agree, but it won't be me." Allison put the book in a bag and handed it to Coraline.

"Why not?"

"Because my focus is on running this bookstore, not on finding a man."

"Well, yes, I can see why that'd be true. It's very important that all the new businesses here on Main Street do well." Coraline cocked her head to the side. "But even successful businesswomen have men in their lives."

"This is the biggest opportunity of my life." Allison straightened some paperwork on the counter. "I can't risk it by losing focus or mooning over Sam."

"Don't you think you might get lonely?"

"With so much to do here and all the people I see when they come in, no, I don't expect so." Maybe down the line, when she'd made this store a success, she could focus a little more on romance. But not for a long while. Her priorities were clear, her prize within sight.

"We shall see, my dear." Coraline put her purse in the crook of her arm. "I'll pray about it for you, all right?"

"All right." A thought occurred to Allison. "Um…I would appreciate it if you could keep all this to yourself. The last thing I want to do is make Sam uncomfortable when he brings the twins back for Story Time." Or to be embarrassed herself if he ever found out about how she'd adored him from afar for so many years.

"I promise I won't say anything."

"Thank you."

Coraline left the store and Allison let out a sigh of relief. Who would have guessed that Coraline had deduced the truth years ago? She was obviously a very wise, intuitive woman.

But she wasn't right about Allison being the Christian woman for Sam. In order to have the life she wanted, she was going to keep Sam in the father-of-Nicky-and-Rosie department and focus strictly on herself. And Happy Endings, of course.

With his last nerve dying a noisy death, Sam herded the twins from the car to the Everything, a gas station/convenience store/grill in town that served burgers, fries and nuked frozen pizza. The place was owned and run by Elwood and Velma Dill, who were self-proclaimed hippies in their early fifties. Elwood was a member of the SOS Committee, and both he and his wife had really become more involved in the community since Randall Manufacturing had closed its doors.

After a long day at work wrangling teenagers and an afternoon spent wrangling the twins, Sam was just too tired to get a meal together. Sometimes it was more work to eat out with the kids. But after the afternoon he'd had at home—which had involved a stray tube of bright red lipstick Teresa had left behind and two rolls of toilet paper unwound all over the house by one mischievous little boy—they all needed a change of scene.

Besides, it was a lovely Indian summer evening, and they should enjoy the nice weather while they could. Soon enough it would be too cold to eat outside. Who knew how Sam would entertain the kids then? Just the thought of being cooped up with them on his own spread little rivers of panic through him. Last winter had been rough, what with his split from Teresa fresh in his mind and his trial-by-fire single parenthood.

"Look, Daddy." Rosie pulled on his hand. "There's the nice story lady."

Sure enough, Allison was sitting at one of the picnic tables set up outside. Another young woman with shoulder-length auburn hair, whom Sam had seen working at the bookstore yesterday, sat across from Allison. The other gal looked familiar, as if he'd seen her around town or something, but he couldn't quite place her.

The sun had begun to set, and the early-evening light glinted off Allison's hair, highlighting it with streaks of gold that perfectly matched the gold-hued coat she wore with a pair of black pants. His heart gave a little blip.

"Yes, there she is," he said, willing himself to ignore the disconcerting effect she had on him.

"Hi, story lady!" Nicky called. "We are here!"

Allison looked their way and froze for just a second. Then her face broke into a big smile. She waved. "Hey, you guys!"

Sam gave a return wave and then let the kids go. They both went scurrying toward Allison, waving as if she were a race-car driver and a fairy princess all wrapped up in one wonderful person.

He followed at a slower pace, trying to look all cool and collected—casual—despite the fact that she hadn't been far from his mind since Story Time yesterday. Her interaction with the twins had had a big impact on him.

No matter how hard he tried, he just couldn't get the picture of her with Rosie out of his mind.

He was a bit in awe of Allison, actually, and that wasn't comfortable; given the female role models he'd had, he hadn't been amazed by any woman for a long time, and the emotion felt foreign and awkward. Guess he'd have to adjust; he should be good at that by now.

Nicky and Rosie were obviously taken with Allison, too. They both hopped around her table, excitedly greeting her as if they were long-lost best friends.

Sam consciously relaxed, then smiled as he drew near. "Well, look here. My kids' favorite person in the whole world."

Allison blushed. "Aw, that's sweet."

"It's true," Rosie said, patting Allison's arm. "You are the bestest story lady ever!"

"She does tell a mean story," the other woman said. She held out her hand with a grin. "Vivian Duncan. I work at the bookstore part-time. I used to work at the library until budget cuts happened." Randall Manufacturing closing had had far-reaching effects on just about everything in town, but especially on town-supported services, like the library, police force and school district.

Sam shook her hand. "Pleased to meet you. Sam Franklin."

Allison blinked. "Oh, where are my manners? I thought you two knew each other."

"Unless it's involved with the high school, I don't get out much." Again, maybe his social life needed to be reworked, although finding the time for any kind of socializing would be a challenge.

"We've never crossed paths, then, even though I've lived in town for quite a while." Viv raised a hand to shield her face from the setting sun. "You guys want to join us?"

Nicky and Rosie squealed. "Yes! We want to!" They both jumped in place.

Sam put a hand on his kids' shoulders and pressed lightly to encourage them to calm down. "Oh, wow, I don't want to intrude."

"Oh, you're not intruding one bit." With a tilt of her head, Viv looked at Allison. "Right, story lady?"

"Right you are, Viv," Allison said, gesturing to the huge pizza with just two slices missing, which sat in the middle of the table. "We ordered a whole pizza, so we've got plenty." The pizzas weren't exactly gourmet. But anything Sam didn't have to make was extra tasty.

"I love pizza," Nicky announced. "I want some."

"Me, too," Rosie added. "The cheesy cheese is good."

"Guys, we can't eat all their food," Sam said.

"Are you kidding?" Allison said. "There's plenty." She smiled at Sam. "Unless you want to add some fries…?"

"Yeah, fries." Nicky rubbed his tummy. "My favorite."

"Well, then, fries it is, if you love them so much," Allison said, then quickly clamped her mouth closed, as if she'd spoken out of turn. "If Dad says it's okay, of course."

"I love them, too, so it's fine," Sam said, unable to say no to his kids. And, really, socializing with a couple of adults sounded good for someone whose day was usually filled with teenagers at work and toddlers at home. Sometimes his brain was mush by dinnertime.

"Great," Allison answered. "Sam, why don't you go order some, and these two kidlets can stay here with us."

"Okay." Sam headed to the order window within earshot to order the fries and some water for him and the twins. There was a short line, so he waited, arms crossed over his chest, and surreptitiously observed the two women and two kids.

Vivian scooted over and patted the bench next to her. "Who wants to sit next to me?"

"I will." Rosie ran over next to Viv, then pointed at Viv's wrist. "Can I look at your bracelet?"

"Sure," Viv said, slipping the bangle off her wrist. "Here you go." She handed it to Rosie.

Rosie eyed it as if it were a priceless piece of jewelry. Sam quirked an eyebrow. His daughter, the jewelry queen. She was a girlie girl for sure. He wondered how he was going to deal with that in the future as a single dad; just the thought of what was to come scared him silly. Dating? Teen angst? *Just kill me now.*

"Well, then, Mr. Nicky, I guess you're stuck with me." Allison moved over. "How about we sit next to each other and you can tell me what you liked most about Mike and Mary Anne."

"Okay," Nicky said. "That was a good story."

She reached out and lifted Nicky onto the bench to sit next to her. Her arm stayed around his little shoulders and she bent her head near to listen to him while he chattered on about the story, his face glowing.

As he waited to order, Sam watched as Allison set paper plates in front of each child with her free hand—multitasking at its finest—and then added a slice of pizza. She even managed to get a napkin on both kids' laps, although Sam knew it wouldn't stay on Nicky's for long; his rambunctious son was usually up and running around the dinner table too much to keep anything on his lap.

Viv and Rosie chatted about Viv's bracelet, and while Viv was obviously a really nice young woman, Sam's eyes kept returning to Allison, to the way the setting sun gilded her cheeks and made her blue eyes glow like a beautiful Caribbean sea. He found himself fascinated with the way she interacted with Nicky, as if he were the most wonderful, interesting little boy in the world, which, of course, he was.

He ordered from Velma, then waited by the window for the food. Once again his gaze was drawn to Allison, who was now playing thumb war with Nicky. Nicky's laughter rang out as he "won" the round, and then he begged Allison to play another match. With a patient smile, Allison obliged.

"Hey, Coach Franklin."

Sam turned. Rory Liston and Scott Martin, two members of the basketball team, stood there, soft drinks in hand. The Everything was something of a teen hangout. "Hey, guys."

"You bring your kids here for dinner?" Rory asked, shoving his shaggy brown hair out of his eyes.

"Yeah, they love going out to eat," Sam replied.

"I love the burgers here," Scott said. "Fries are pretty good, too." Scott wasn't as tall as Rory and was a bit huskier. He wore his blond hair in a buzz cut, and he always wore a baseball cap, backward most of the time.

"Yeah," Rory said, jabbing an elbow in Scott's side. "You always eat all of them." The two boys had grown up together and were as close as brothers.

"You're the one who needs all the grease in them," Scott said. Rory was a tall kid and as skinny as a beanpole.

"He'll fill out eventually," Sam said. "I was pretty lean in my youth, too."

"Yeah, my dad said he was as skinny as me when he was my age," Rory said. "And he's all muscle now." Rory's dad, Vern, had been on the Bygones police force for years, but had lost his job recently due to budget cuts brought on when Randall Manufacturing had closed its doors. Sam had a feeling Rory was struggling with more than just his falling grades, which was one of the reasons

Sam hoped Rory would be willing to attend Allison's creative-writing workshops.

"Coach, your order's ready," Velma said. She had a colorful scarf wrapped around her neck and some kind of feather thingies hanging in her long hair, which she had pulled back at her nape.

"Great." Sam picked up the fries and drinks. "Thanks, Velma." He turned his gaze to the two boys. "You two stay out of trouble, all right?"

Both Rory and Scott nodded. "Sure thing, Coach."

Man, he never got tired of being called Coach. He loved working with kids, influencing them to make good choices. "See you at practice tomorrow after school." Sam carried the order back to the table and set it down. "Fry alert," he announced.

With happy squeals, the kids dug in.

Sam scrunched in next to Allison, his leg lightly touching hers under the small table that was obviously designed for four regular-size people and not four plus one six-foot-three-inch man. She didn't try to scoot away, so he tried not to let her proximity get to him. However, obviously Allison wasn't a kid anymore; she was an attractive woman. He'd have to have ice water in his veins not to notice that.

Nicky and Rosie kept eating the fries with gusto, holding up each one before they ate it to compare the length; it was a game they played in search of the longest one.

Sam helped himself to a slice of pizza, having to touch Allison's arm in the process, and his breathing hitched just a bit at the contact. To cover up his reaction, he started munching on his pizza.

"Do you ever feed them?" Allison said with a slanted eyebrow, her eyes on the fry-eating machines.

"Once in a while, when I remember," he quipped before he popped a fry in his mouth.

"These are yummy," Rosie said, dipping a fry in ketchup, then gobbling it up.

"Okay, I have to try one of these delish fries," Allison said, picking one up. She held it up. "Okay, kids, with ketchup or without?"

"With!" Nicky and Rosie said in unison.

Allison dipped and then made a big show of eating.

"Sam, you might have to get another order," Viv said.

"I was just thinking the same thing," he replied. He eyed the pizza. "Doesn't look like they're interested in that right now." He got up and ordered some more fries.

The lively conversation kept up while everyone ate, and Sam found himself very conscious of the woman sitting next to him. Allison laughed and joked around with the kids, and had them both giggling with her stories about Sam when he was a teenager.

Toward the end of the meal, she gently wiped Nicky's pizza hands and ketchup-ringed mouth with a napkin. Sam watched, impressed; her motherly streak with someone else's children was something to behold.

When the pile of fries and three-quarters of the pizza were gone and the kids were relatively clean, he, Viv and Allison started clearing the table. Nicky and Rosie chased each other, pretending they were wild puppies.

Allison looked at them. "It would be a really nice night for a trip to Bronson Park to play, don't you think?" Bronson Park, named for the two Bronson brothers who'd founded the town, was located just behind the Everything and had an old-fashioned gazebo, playground, basketball court and a pond complete with numerous duck families.

"I love the park!" Nicky said between play woofs as he ran by. "Let's go!"

"Me, too." Rosie clapped as she ran by, hot on Nicky's heels, Viv's bracelet glinting on her upper arm. "I want to swing."

"Well, then, let's go," Allison said. "If it's okay with your dad."

He looked at his watch; the twins' bedtime was creeping up fast. "I don't know…"

"Tired kids are happy kids, and that makes for a happy parent," Allison said. "Besides, after a long day at work, I could use a turn on the swings myself. How about you, Viv?"

"Unfortunately, I'm going to have to take a rain check," Viv replied. "I have some paperwork at home I have to get done tonight."

Allison's eyes widened. "Oh, okay." After an awkward pause, she regarded Sam, her hands shoved into the back pockets of her jeans. "So. How about it?" Her gaze strayed to the human puppies. "Looks like the kids could use a trip to the park to burn off some energy."

He paused for a second. He usually stuck pretty close to the children's schedule when he had them, firmly believing a strict routine was better for everyone. But they *were* pretty wound up right now, and some extra playtime would probably mean a quieter night later on. Was there a better reason for accepting Allison's invitation?

"Sure, we can go for a while," he said, telling himself his agreement was all about the kids having fun and tuckering themselves out.

And had nothing whatsoever to do with wanting to spend more time with one all-grown-up and very intriguing Allison True.

Chapter Four

"Look how high I can go!" Nicky squealed. "Higher, higher!"

"I can go as high as Nicky," Rosie cried. "Higher, Daddy, higher."

Sam gave Rosie another push, then gave Allison a wry smile. "Looks like we have ourselves a little competition here."

She pushed Nicky and returned Sam's smile. "When you were a kid, did you ever wish you could go so high you'd go all the way around on the swing?"

"Of course." He pushed Rosie again, a bit harder, yet still lightly. In actuality, they weren't going high at all, except from a three-year-old's perspective. "Doesn't everybody wish that?"

"Good point," Allison replied. "The swings were always my favorite. The monkey bars came in a close second."

"I always liked the slide," Sam replied. "We used to have races to see who could get in the most trips down during recess."

"We did that, too," Allison said. A breeze kicked up and blew her long, dark hair around her face. Between pushing Nicky, she tried to corral the errant strands.

Sam couldn't help but notice her profile, complete with perfect nose and high cheekbones. She really was pretty, but her appeal went much deeper than simple good looks. He'd seen through her interactions with the twins that Allison possessed a kind and good heart, as well as a compassionate nature.

"Daddy, I'm gonna play in the sandbox," Rosie said, pointing at the large, wood-sided sandbox embedded in the grass to their left.

He caught her and stopped her forward motion. "Okay, honey. You want to go play in the sandbox, Nicky?" Gingerly, he lifted her off the swing.

"Yes, sandbox!" Nicky shouted.

"Okay, bud." Allison grabbed Nicky and brought him to a stop and lifted him to the ground. "There you go."

Both kids ran off and plunked themselves down in the sandbox.

Sam turned to Allison and an idea hit him. "You want me to push you on the swing?"

"I thought you'd never ask." With a bright smile, she went around to the front of the swing and sat down in the black rubber seat. "Let's make this baby fly," she said, looking back over her shoulder at him, her eyes sparkling like ocean-blue jewels. She flicked her feet at the cedar chips on the ground to get herself moving. "Maybe I'll go all the way around!"

Her excitement was contagious. "Let's see what we can do about that." As she swung backward, he grabbed the swing's chains down low and pulled, putting his back into it. "Here we go."

She was light as a feather, so it wasn't hard

to pull her up and back a long way, until her feet were off the ground. He held her there and leaned in close to her. "You ready?"

She bounced in the seat. "Ready."

Just then, the wind blew her silky hair across his face. He froze, and the subtle scent of peaches surrounded him for a second. Instantly his knees went weak. For just a moment he had the undeniable urge to bend even closer and bury his face in that soft, fragrant mass of hair.

"Sam?" She quickly turned.

He couldn't back up, and they ended up face-to-face, only inches apart. She froze, her lips slack, her blue gaze wide. He was so close he could see the light gray flecks in her eyes.

So close he'd only have to move a little bit and he'd be kissing her....

That stunning thought knocked some sense into him. With a remarkable amount of smoothness, considering the situation, he backed up a bit and gave her a smile, hoping he looked calm, cool and collected when he felt anything but. "Here we go." He somehow managed to sound carefree, not strangled and flustered. Good. He could do suave. Kind of.

With a burst of power he pulled her up higher and then let her go.

She swung forward, pumping her legs and leaning back in perfect playground-swing style. Then she made the trip backward, her feet tucked underneath her as she leaned slightly forward. At just the right moment, honed from years on the playground as a kid, he firmly but gently pushed her slim back and she sailed forward, her hair flying behind her.

A crystal-clear laugh rang out and his breath caught in his chest at the pure sound of joy echoing in the evening air. He smiled, her delight his, her blithe happiness filtering into his blood. And so it went, her swinging back with him pushing her, establishing the perfect cadence, a perfect connection, no words needed. Swing. Push. Repeat.

He glanced at the sandbox to be sure the twins were okay. They were both seated in the sand, happily playing away, so Sam kept pushing. Soon Allison swung almost parallel with the top bar of the swing's frame, so much so that she was starting to drop on her way back toward him instead of swinging smoothly. She let out a squeal, and suddenly he worried it was a fearful squeal rather than a delighted one, that she was soaring too high too fast. So on her next swing back, he acted on instinct and grabbed her around her slender waist.

Once he had a hold on her, he ran to stop her forward progress. "Whoa, there."

She came to a jerky stop. Safe and sound. Unable to help himself, he left his arms around her, his head tucked in close to her shoulder from the back for just a moment. The fresh, fruity smell of her hair blasted him again, along with the feel of her so tantalizingly close to him. The now-familiar knee weakness hit him so hard he almost stumbled. By sheer will he pulled back and kept himself from face planting at her feet.

She giggled. "Wow, that was so much fun," she said, turning, her face glowing rosy pink, her wind-tossed hair tumbling down around her shoulders. "It's amazing how something as simple as a swing on a playground can make all my cares just disappear."

"I was just thinking the same thing." He smiled, trying not to stare at the pretty picture she made with the green grass as the perfect backdrop for her quiet yet disarming beauty. "Great minds, right?"

She stood. "Oh, definitely." A slender eyebrow went up and she gestured to the swing. "You want a turn? It's even better from there."

He didn't know how the experience could be better than watching her fly, hearing her laugh and having her hair close enough to smell. But he couldn't say that without looking foolish. However, the thought of having her hands on his back, of sharing his delight with her, beckoned like an impossible dream. One he hadn't allowed in a very long time.

For good reason.

Instantly reality crashed down on his head and he thought about soaring too high too fast. Not a good plan. Better to stay safe. Contained. In control. In all aspects of his life. He opened his mouth to reply, "no, thanks," only to be interrupted by Rosie's shriek. "Daddy! Nicky *throwed* sand on me!"

Sam darted his gaze to the sandbox. Rosie still sat there, only now huge globs of sand were stuck to her dark hair. Nicky stood in the grass, his eyes reflecting a mulish light.

Sam held up a hand to Allison. "Excuse me." He went over to the sandbox. "Is this true, Nicky? Did you throw sand on your sister?" Sam asked in a stern voice.

"Ro-ro's tryin' to boss me," Nicky said, his lower lip sticking out in a pronounced pout, which Sam knew was a sure sign of guilt in Nicky.

"He stealed my sand," Rosie said with a glower of her own as she gestured to the whole sandbox. Obviously she thought every grain of sand was hers. Sam sighed. They'd need to work on sharing. A lot.

"My sand." Nicky pointed at Rosie with a rigid finger.

Rosie bossing and Nicky reacting like this was a familiar skirmish, and Sam was growing tired of the conflict, especially when it involved silly things like sand. He did his best to keep his patience. "Hey, now, you two, let's calm down. There's enough sand for everyone." Sounded logical.

Nicky bent and picked up a handful of sand. "My sand," he said again, holding his hand up, obviously getting ready to hurl it at Rosie again.

"Nicky, do not throw that sand at your sister," Sam commanded, shaking a finger.

Nicky wound up—

"Nicky?" Allison called. "How about I push you on the swing?"

Nicky's gaze swung toward Allison just as Sam's did.

"Swing?" Nicky asked, lowering his fistful of sand.

"Sure." Allison crooked a finger. "I'd love to give you a fun ride, with my very special touch."

Nicky dropped the sand at his feet, on to more attractive things, apparently. "Okay. I am special." He ran to the swings and held up his arms to Allison. "Help me up."

Figuratively, Sam's jaw fell. Allison made refereeing the kids look so easy. So second nature for her. He looked at her, blinking, feeling like the parenting idiot Teresa always accused him of being.

As she lifted Nicky into the swing, she mouthed the word *distraction*.

"Ah," he murmured. Smart woman. He needed to pay attention to her. Should be easy, considering how much he enjoyed being around her. And the twins. They enjoyed her, too.

Sam sat down on the edge of the sandbox and played with Rosie as she shaped sand into mountains. He kept one eye on Allison and Nicky—well, maybe both eyes, but who was keeping score?

In no time at all Allison had Nicky gently swinging, with a few easy spins thrown in for that special touch she spoke about. Nicky giggled and kicked his feet in obvious delight.

Just about the time Rosie had her third mountain completed, she started to whine and rub her eyes with the backs of her hands. Tiredness was setting in after their fun evening, and the kids' bedtime was looming.

Time to go. He only hoped he could get Nicky out of the park without a tantrum.

Sam stood. "I think it's time to head home, kids."

Nicky howled. *"Nooo!"* There it was, his usual reaction—argue and throw a fit. "I want to stay!" His face reddened and Sam knew tears would be next; Nicky was nothing if not predictable. Sam's brain scrambled for a way to deal with his son's behavior. Cajoling? Bribery? Discipline? Nothing much worked reliably, and he was out of ideas.

Before he could come up with a plan, Allison caught the swing and stopped Nicky. "Are you sure? 'Cause if you cooperate with your dad, I'll give you a piggyback ride to the car."

"Piggyback?" Nicky said.

"You bet," Allison replied. "But you have to mind your dad, all right?"

"Okay." Appeased, Nicky scooted out of the swing and held his arms up. "I love piggyback."

Sam was dumbfounded.

Allison knelt. "Okay, then, Mr. Nicky." She

gestured to her back. "Climb on and maybe we can pretend I'm your horse."

"Me, too." Rosie clambered to her feet, smashing one of her carefully crafted sand mountains in the process. "I want a horsey piggyback, Daddy."

"Okay, Rosie." He knelt and crouched way down. "Get on my back and maybe we can race Miss Allison and Nicky."

"Race!" Rosie crowed as she crawled onto his back. "I will win!"

"Yeah, we race!" Nicky squealed, clearly willing to go with the flow for something fun. Wasn't it amazing how fast toddlers' attention shifted when presented with entertaining options? Allison was a master at that tactic, whereas he usually just did what his own dad had done and imposed his will on them. Not that Dad was ever mean or abusive, but it had been clear who was boss in the Franklin household.

Allison's approach was clearly better, and he marveled at her creativity in dealing with the twins. He'd better pay attention.

He rose, and Allison moved over next to

him with Nicky on her back. "Okay, are you two ready for a race?" she asked with a brilliant smile that had Sam's heart twitching.

"I'm ready!" Nicky kicked his feet at Allison's hips. "Let's go."

"I'm ready, too," Rosie announced, bouncing on Sam's back like a real cowgirl. "Go!"

Sam looked at Allison. "You ready?"

Suddenly, she jerked sideways and started running. "See ya later!" she yelled over Nicky's squeals.

Dead surprise froze Sam for a few seconds. Why, that little schemer, she'd jumped the gun.

"Run, Daddy, run!" Rosie said, kicking her legs at his sides.

Belatedly, he broke into a trot as he tightened his hands on Rosie's lower legs to hold her in place. "Hold on, Rosie-girl! I'm gonna have to run fast to catch up."

Rosie giggled and bounced. "Okay, Daddy! Geeyup!" she said, mangling *giddyup* in her cute little way.

He moved along as fast as he could, but Allison had a pretty good head start and seemed to have the whole piggyback-horsey thing down to a science. She ran smoothly yet with purpose, keeping Nicky firmly on her back, whereas Sam had to slow down to keep Rosie from tumbling off.

How did Allison do that?

By the time he reached the edge of the park, which bordered the parking lot of the Everything, Allison was already around the corner, presumably reaching his car in record time.

He picked up the pace as he hit the parking lot, squeezing Rosie's legs harder, hoping to make up time with a final push. But, sure enough, as he rounded the corner, he saw Allison and Nicky reach the car. Nicky's shrieks of glee echoed in the dusk-tinged air.

A few seconds later, Sam arrived at the race finish, breathing hard. Rosie was giggling so much she seemed incapable of speaking. Nicky was bouncing on Allison's back, his face split into a delight-fueled smile.

Allison appeared barely winded.

"You jumped the gun," Sam managed to say, hiking Rosie up higher on his back. "And you've clearly had piggyback horse races before."

"You've got me there." Allison inclined her head to the side and flashed him an impish grin. "I did this all the time when my sisters were little."

"I'd say that's an unfair advantage," he replied, returning her smile, unable to resist her teasing demeanor. "We'll have to have a rematch."

"O-okay." She paused, then looked pointedly at Rosie. "Although next time I may let you guys win for a different reason."

Catching her drift, he nodded knowingly as his chest squeezed. "Good idea."

He unlocked the SUV, and Allison efficiently helped him load the kids into their car seats. She kept up a steady stream of lighthearted conversation about nothing in particular with both children as they went about getting everyone settled.

Just as she finished buckling the Y strap over Nicky's head, he reached out his chubby arms and hugged her. "Thank you, Miss Allison."

She hugged him back, her mouth curved into a gentle smile that had Sam staring for just a moment. "You're welcome, sweetie pie." She pulled back and held up a hand with her palm toward Nicky. "And good work with your cooperating. I'm pretty sure your dad appreciates it a lot." As Nicky slapped her hand, she looked at Sam across the backseat and winked.

He winked back. "You've got that right," he replied. And the more he was around Allison, the more he appreciated *her*. In a good-friend kind of way.

"I like to o'operate," Nicky said.

"Me, too," Rosie added.

"Good." Allison backed out of her position, slammed the door with a final wave to Nicky and made her way around the SUV to where Sam stood. "Don't close that door. I need to hug your daughter."

He stepped back and gestured to Rosie. "Be my guest."

Allison bent and gave Rosie a hug. "Bye-bye, Rosie-roo."

Rosie giggled. "I'm Rosie-roo." She patted

Allison's face. "Will you come play with us in the park again?"

"I'd like to," Allison replied, squeezing Rosie's hand. "Maybe next time I can be your piggyback horsey." She paused, then added, "If it's okay with your daddy."

"Okay," Rosie said on a yawn.

Sam figured she was plumb tuckered out after their dinner out and playtime with Allison. Hopefully, Nicky was, too, and bedtime would be easy; after the kids went to sleep, Sam still had a lot of homework to grade, and he also had work to do on the new curriculum for his calculus class. He'd be happy to be in bed by midnight.

Allison straightened and stood.

Sam shut the door of the SUV and looked at her. "You've got quite a way with them."

Allison shrugged. "I love children."

"I can tell." She was going to make some kids one fantastic mother someday. "They really like you."

She looked over his shoulder and waved at the kidlets one more time. "They're fantastic children, Sam."

"Well, thank you." He cleared his throat. "Sometimes I have my doubts about how good of a job I'm doing."

"Three-year-olds are notoriously challenging," she said with a sympathetic look.

"Maybe," he said. "I just feel like I can't do anything right." Teresa shared the sentiment. Or at least made him think she did. Her way of keeping him in line? Maybe. She used manipulation all the time. But when his kids were at stake, he had to pay attention.

Allison touched his arm, creating a warm spot clear to the bone. "I think most parents in your position feel like they're floundering."

"I guess you're right." He studied her. "They seem to listen to you more."

"You mean o'operate?" she asked with a quirk of an eyebrow.

"Exactly," he replied.

"Well, I'm sure it's just because I'm novel, and that's always fun. You, on the other hand, are old news to them, and you're the rule enforcer by necessity. Don't be too hard on yourself."

"I'll try not to be," he said, appreciating her

viewpoint, which was so different from what he usually heard.

An awkward silence ensued.

Allison spoke first. "Well, it's been very nice seeing you again, Sam. I've been working really hard to the exclusion of just about everything else, so it feels good to reconnect with an old friend."

Old friend. Right. Perfect. "Yeah, it has."

"Okay, so I'll see you tomorrow. At Story Time." She gave him a wave. "Bye."

"Bye."

He watched her walk away. The wind blew her hair around, and he thought of how soft it had felt against his face, like fresh peaches wrapped in silk. In a few moments she disappeared around the corner.

He climbed into the SUV's driver's seat and, with his hands on the steering wheel, sat for a long minute, deep in thought. He sure liked how Allison interacted with Nicky and Rosie. She was fantastic with them. So he'd take them to Story Time tomorrow. But that would be it. His divorce had taught him he just wasn't cut out for love.

Chapter Five

The day after she played in the park with Sam and the kids, Allison left Viv out in the store in the morning and sequestered herself in the tiny room that served as her office. She was in charge of everything that went with running a retail store, and lately, the inventory-control software had been giving her fits.

Josh Smith, who owned the Cozy Cup Café and was also a computer guru of sorts, had helped her set up the whole computer system and software when the store had opened in July. She'd thought she had a pretty good handle on the system lately, but the inventory-control program hadn't been loading properly. With her high-tech thinking cap on, she hunched over the desktop that took up most of her desk and did her best to figure out what was wrong.

All she ended up with was less hair. So at lunchtime, needing a break and some fresh air, she stretched, told Viv she'd be back soon and headed to the Cozy Cup to ask Josh if he'd have time soon to take a look at the system. She wasn't above asking for help; she'd do it all day if it meant making the business run smoother. The last thing she needed was a hinky computer system causing problems.

She found Josh behind the counter at the Cozy Cup, dressed in jeans, a red shirt and an apron with the Cozy Cup logo on the front. He was a tall man with dark red hair and green eyes, somewhere in his midtwenties. In Allison's opinion he was extremely intelligent, if a bit nerdy in a let-me-fix-your-computer kind of way, and was also clearly very enterprising.

"Hey, Josh." She looked around, taking note of the small glass-topped tables scattered about. "You've done such a wonderful job here." He sold pastries from Sweet Dreams Bakery, along with coffee and tea.

"Thanks," he said. "I've been meaning to come by the bookstore and order a few books to keep on the bookshelves I'm going to install in the next week or so."

"Excellent," she said. "If you don't mind, I'll put together a list of my favorites that you might want to include."

He nodded. "You're the literature expert, so I'll welcome the advice."

She beamed. Literature expert. Wow. "Great. Maybe I can ask you for the same."

"Shoot," he said, drying off one of the coffee cups sitting on the counter in front of him.

"I'm having a terrible time with the inventory-control software, and I was wondering if you could see your way over sometime in the next day or so to help me figure out what's wrong."

"Of course," he said. "I love computer challenges."

"Yes, well, I don't, so I'd appreciate any help you can give."

He promised to stop by soon, and then after

serving her a to-go cup of his lovely signature roast, she left to walk back to Happy Endings.

She strolled along the wide sidewalk of Main Street, taking in the sights, loving the old-fashioned look of downtown Bygones. Wrought-iron lampposts marched down the street, and matching benches dotted the sidewalk, providing a nice place to sit for anyone needing a break while shopping. Big clay pots filled with large evergreens also sat here and there, adding a wonderful sense of texture and color to the street. The tan buildings, which she knew had been built in the 1930s, were in good condition and sported colorful awnings and nicely painted contrasting door frames, which contributed a wonderful, welcoming ambience to the town.

She still couldn't believe she owned a business here. In her hometown, on this perfect street. She was so blessed, so fortunate. She had to make Happy Endings a success.

She returned to the store and received a delivery of books, and then spent an hour or so unloading and shelving them with Viv. They discussed changing the layout of the fiction section of the store, but decided to leave things be for the time being until they had a better idea of what was selling and what wasn't.

Joe Sheridan, the chief of police and also a member of the SOS Committee, stopped by midafternoon.

"Hello, Miss True." He sported a dark blond crew cut and wore the blue jeans and chambray shirt uniform of the Bygones Police Department. He also had a pair of sunglasses hanging from his breast pocket, which was emblazoned with the police department logo. She'd guess he was in his midforties.

"Well, hello, Chief Sheridan." She came out from behind the counter. "Everything all right?" She hoped he wasn't here on any kind of police business.

"Oh, yeah, everything's fine. I just wanted to pick out a book for my wife, Inez, who's feeling poorly with a cold. She's really into medical thrillers. What do you recommend?"

"I have some excellent new titles that just came in." She crooked a hand and gestured to the fiction section. "Why don't you come back here and I'll show you some of my favorites?"

After much discussion, the chief picked two titles by a relatively new author and then followed her to the register. As she rang up the books, he looked around. "You've done a great job here." He got out his wallet. "How's business?"

"It's all right," she said. "Things have picked up a little in the past few weeks." But not enough. Yet. "That'll be sixteen dollars."

He dug out some bills. "I was just talking to Mayor Langston about how the success of the new businesses is so important to Bygones."

"Yes, I agree. And I've been working long hours to make sure I pull my end." In fact, twelve-hour days were the norm right now. Her night with Sam and the twins had been the first one in many that she hadn't worked straight through until midnight.

"Excellent. The schools and police force still aren't safe, so we on the SOS Committee appreciate your hard work."

Which meant Sam's job was at risk, along with a lot of other jobs in town, too, and, hence, the very lifeblood of Bygones. "I'll do whatever necessary to make sure Happy Endings is around for a very long time to come, Chief." She put the books in a bag, which had the Happy Endings loaded-bookshelf logo she'd designed on it, and handed it to him, along with his receipt.

"That's why we chose you, Allison. And just between you and me, you also have a history here in town that gave you an edge over some of the other applicants. We're confident you'll make this store work."

Pride spread through her. "Well, I'm grateful for the opportunity, believe me." She'd been given a once-in-a-lifetime chance, and she wouldn't squander it. "I won't let the committee or the town down."

With a wave and a hearty thank-you, the chief left, and Allison went back to work with Viv for the rest of the afternoon. She lost herself in straightening, helping customers and fiddling with some accounts-payable paperwork she'd started at about eleven o'clock last night.

She'd just gone out front when she spied

Sam and the twins walking into the store a few minutes before Story Time began. She paused for a second, and then moved out from behind the counter and made her way over to the Franklin family. Sam wore well-fitting black sweatpants and a red fitted athletic long-sleeved T-shirt that really showed off his muscular upper arms.

She noted in what she told herself was a very analytical way that he'd definitely filled out in the ten years since she'd seen him, though he was still tall, lean and fit.

"Hey, Nicky and Rosie!" she called, waving. Sam and the twins were now making a beeline for the Kids' Korner, with Nicky leading the way.

The three of them turned. The twins smiled and so did Sam, flashing white teeth that lit up his face like a ray of sunshine had burned a hole in the roof and hit his mouth just so. She half expected those teeth to glint with an exploding star, cartoon style. Boy, was he handsome.

Nicky and Rosie ran to her. "Miss Allison!" they crowed. "We are here!" Two sets of chubby arms went around her knees.

She pressed a hand to the back of each dark head and her heart turned to mush. "I see that. Just in time for the story." She'd picked out two stories specifically with them in mind, one about a race car and his vehicle buddies and one about a certain princess named Rapunzel.

"Car story?" Nicky asked.

"No, no, Nicky." Rosie wagged a finger at her brother in what Allison was beginning to think of as her signature move. "Princess story."

Nicky shoved out his chin. "Car story, Ro-ro!"

Another finger wag. "Princess!" Rosie barked.

"Car!" Nicky retorted, lifting hand towards Rosie's ponytail.

Allison quickly put herself between the two kids as she looked at Sam and gave him an amused grin. He rolled his eyes and grimaced in a vague semblance of a grin; clearly, dealing with the twins' discordant dynamic day after day got old fast.

She gave them a stern look. "Don't worry, I have stories for both of you two munchkins. As soon as you quit bickering and sit down and become story listeners, we'll get started."

The kids took the bait, and ran over to the story rug, plopping down next to the other two kids who'd already taken a seat.

Sam moved nearer, and she caught the scent of something spicy and masculine. Warm and rich. Aftershave? She hadn't smelled that yesterday....

"More like story arguers," he said, his eyes tinged with embarrassment. "I'm sorry for that little skirmish."

She discreetly sidled backward, hopefully out of smelling range. Why torture herself? "Don't apologize. They're little kids. It would be weird if they behaved perfectly."

He ran a hand through his hair. "I dunno..." His jaw tightened and he shook his head.

"Trust me, they're fine. And normal. I can't tell you how many fights I broke up between my little sisters over the years." Allison had regularly mediated between her siblings. In her parents' absence, she became an expert at keeping the peace in the True household.

Sam's face softened and his rich dark gaze roamed over her face. "How is it that you always make me feel better?"

She blinked, speechless. She somehow found her voice. "Um…well, I'm not quite s-sure," she stammered. She was certain she had a flashing neon sign on her forehead that read FLUSTERED. She had to find a way to handle that reaction or she'd die of embarrassment before the week was out.

"Well, you do, and I appreciate it." He gestured to the twins, who were sitting quietly on the rug without arguing or even speaking, their temporary halos firmly in place. "And so do the other kids and parents here for Story Time."

His heartfelt praise had a rosy flush spreading through Allison. "I'm just glad I could help." She managed to sound normal this time. Good, she could keep Sam where he needed to be.

Then her eyes caught in Sam's gaze and

she froze, staring. Her tummy flipped, her heart rate sped up and for the life of her she couldn't look away.

"Miss Allison?" Nicky's voice jerked Allison back to reality.

She broke the visual connection with Sam and looked at Nicky. "Er, yes, Nicky?" Allison said, trying to make her voice sound normal.

"We waiting quietly for the story," Nicky said.

"Why, yes, you are, sweetie." Allison cleared her throat. What was wrong with her? "Good job." She glanced at Sam. "Um, I'm going to read." She avoided looking directly into his eyes again and then moved past him to the story rug. The scent of his aftershave wafted by again, and her heart gave another blip.

She gritted her teeth and willed her pulse back under control. Sternly she reminded herself that getting hung up on Sam again was not an option. She wasn't in the market for a man—she was in the market for a successful business; a healthy Bygones, which she'd been entrusted to help bring about; and saving her own self-worth by making Happy Endings a resounding success for years to come.

And that was more than enough for her any way she cut it.

Sam sat in an adult chair while Allison talked to the kids before she started the story.

He'd been well aware of his and Allison's little eye lock just now, and he was determined to pass it off as his natural reaction to an attractive young woman. No harm in that, as long as he didn't get carried away.

He wasn't ready for any kind of romance, what with the turmoil in his family right now. All he wanted to do was focus on his job and the kids, and keep his heart out of the whole thing.

Just as Allison started the story, his cell phone vibrated in his pocket. He stood and headed away from the Kids' Korner to take the call as he looked at the screen. Teresa. He tightened his jaw reflexively.

He pressed Talk. "Hello?"

"Hey, it's me."

"Yes?" Given how his and Teresa's marriage had ended, their relationship remained strained, and probably always would. He wasn't going to lie; he was still bitter. Normally, he'd count on God to help him with that problem. But lately, he and God hadn't been that close.

"Listen, Spense and I have decided to go out of town for a few days."

"What?" Sam gripped his cell phone hard. "I'm supposed to drop the kids off in less than an hour." He and Teresa had an every-other-week shared-custody arrangement, and on his week, she watched the kids during the day while he worked.

"I know, but Spense really needs to get away."

"Spense needs to get away?" Sam resisted the urge to laugh. He needed to get away, too, and had since his marriage had gone south. But that wasn't going to happen anytime soon.

"Well, yes. You know how much pressure he's been under at work."

Sam wanted to laugh; he'd heard through the grapevine that the attorney only worked four days a week and played golf at least two afternoons a week. "What do you expect me to do with the kids?"

"Can't you find someone else to watch them? What about Lori?"

Sam squeezed the space between his nose and his eyes, wondering where the old Teresa had gone, the one he'd fallen in love with in college. That seemed like a lifetime ago. She'd turned into a self-centered mess. Perhaps he'd only seen what he wanted to see back then. Honestly, though, motherhood had never agreed with her, and if not for Sam, he knew now she probably wouldn't have had kids at all. "Lori is out of town at Jeff's insurance conference and Dad's still fighting that flu bug going around."

"How about Mrs. Jamison?" Delores Jamison was Sam's neighbor.

"She's eighty, Teresa, and you know she broke her hip three months ago. She can't watch the kids anymore. They'd run circles around her."

"Oh, yeah. I forgot."

Convenient. Teresa only remembered things when it made her life easier. He switched the phone to his other ear. "I was counting on you."

"Well, I'm sorry, but I'm not going to be available for the rest of the week." A male voice said something in the background. Spense. Teresa paused, then went on. "Listen, I have to go or we'll miss our flight."

This kind of move was so Teresa; she'd become even more flaky ever since she'd met Spense. "And you just had to wait until the last minute to tell me? I have to be at practice at five-fifteen."

"These plans were sudden or I would have called you sooner."

Sam bit his cheek, determined not to stoop to her level. "Fine.

"When will you be back?"

"I'm not sure."

Sam didn't think he could trust himself to be civil, so he held his tongue and retorted, "Let me know when you come home."

"I will," she said. "Goodbye, Sam."

Sam clicked off and then stood for a moment, looking at the floor, feeling his pulse surging in his head. Teresa was impossible, and she had him over a barrel. That was reality, and he had to accept it, or go crazy.

In the here and now, though, what was he going to do? He'd been counting on Teresa to watch the kids during practice, and with basketball season just about to start, he couldn't afford to miss a practice.

And, really, he didn't want to disappoint the boys on the team. As was the case in many small towns, sports were a big deal in Bygones, and was often all that was going on for teens at any given time. If not for practice after school, who knew what the kids would be up to. Trouble, probably.

But…he was out of options. He clenched his teeth and shook his head. Looked like he'd have to cancel practice. And hope he could make arrangements for someone to watch the twins tomorrow and Friday.

"Sam, is everything all right?"

He turned. Allison stood holding the book

she'd been reading. Her normally smooth brow was creased.

"Oh, yeah." He waved a hand in the air to emphasize his point. "Everything's good." He didn't want to dump his ex-wife and day-care problems on her.

"Everything doesn't look good." She moved closer, her head canted to the side. "Your jaw's so tight it looks like it's going to crack."

He abruptly unclenched his teeth and held up his cell phone. "I just got off the phone with Teresa, and she has a way of making me tense." Understatement.

"What did she want?" Allison said, then immediately clapped her hand over her mouth. "Oops, sorry. It's none of my business."

"No, it's okay." He let out a heavy breath. He needed to commiserate. "She called to tell me she's going out of town and won't be able to watch the twins while I'm at practice."

"Oh, I'm so sorry."

"Yeah, and it's going to be a big problem for me to find someone else on such short notice." He chewed on his cheek. "I guess I'll have to cancel practice."

"Is there someone else who can watch them?"

He shook his head. "Nope. Lori is out of town and my dad has the flu."

Allison paused. "I could watch them."

He blinked. "No, absolutely not. I don't want to impose."

"It wouldn't be an imposition. Viv's here, and I can entertain the kids in the Kids' Korner." Allison smiled. "That's what it's for."

"I guess so…" He turned over all his options, which were few. Maybe his teenage neighbor, Shawna, could babysit…. No, she was on the girls' soccer team, and they were at an away game this afternoon. Lori, no. Dad, no. Shawna, no. Three strikes. And out.

He put his hands on his hips and looked at Allison, mulling. He had no qualms with how the kids would fare; she was good with them and they loved her. To them, she was like the circus and Sesame Street all rolled into one fun, loving package. And to him—

"Come up with anything?" Allison asked

with a lift of her brow. "You look pretty deep in thought there."

"No." He was stuck. "You sure you don't mind?"

"Absolutely not. They're great kids, Sam. It'll be fun."

His rational side made him throw out one last-ditch effort to give her an out. "As you know, Nicky can be a bit of a handful, and Rosie, well, she's pretty bossy."

Allison shook her head, her eyes sparkling. "I can handle them just fine, so don't worry. I wrangled my little sisters all the time, so there isn't anything Rosie and Nicky could throw at me that I haven't already dealt with."

"If you're sure…"

"I am, so go to your practice, take your time and come back and get the kids here when you're done."

"Okay." What other viable choice did he have on such short notice? "How about I bring burgers from the Everything and we can have dinner?"

"That would be great. We'll all be starved by then." She smoothed a lock of hair behind her ear. "And I'm guessing the kids will be thrilled about the burgers."

"And dinner is the least I can do to thank you for your help. Although, you'll really deserve combat pay."

She waved a hand in the air. "Oh, pshaw. Being with your kids is never a hardship, trust me."

"Okay, I will trust you." He really thought highly of her generosity, her no-nonsense approach to the twins and how she thought they could do no wrong, even though he knew better. "If Nicky gets out of hand—"

"Sam, don't worry. We'll be fine. Go," she said, shooing him away as she moved closer. "I'm happy to watch them whenever you need me."

The faint scent of peaches wafted his way, tantalizing him. He tried to focus on their conversation. He was out of options. "If you're sure."

"As long as you come back bearing burgers, we'll be good," she said. "And fries, too."

She didn't ask for much. "I'm going," he said, finally capitulating. "Practice ends at seven, and I'll be back as soon as I pick up the food."

"The store closes at seven, so just knock and I'll let you in."

"Sounds good." He spontaneously touched her arm and squeezed, leaving his hand there for a moment. Warmth seeped into his fingers. "And thank you again. You've really rescued me from a bind. The guys on the team thank you, too."

She gave him a smile, her lips trembling. "It's no big deal."

"It is to me." He turned and headed toward the front of the store, then reversed course. "Where is my brain?" Caught up in Allison? "I'd better go say goodbye to the kids."

"I've got another story to read, so make it quick," she said, shooing him playfully.

He saluted. "Yes, ma'am."

He went back and said goodbye, and they were thrilled that they were going to get to stay at Miss Allison's for a few more hours, and both seemed comfortable with the change in plans. Thankfully, they weren't clingy kids. They were already engrossed in books that made sounds when he headed back to the front door.

Allison followed him. "See you in a few hours."

He opened the door and turned, his hand on the knob. She regarded him with eyes made bright blue by the muted outside light shining through the open door. His breath stalled like a floating jump shot from the three-point line, and he had to will himself not to gawk like a hormone-fueled teenager. Somehow, he managed to speak. "I owe you."

"Stop," she said, shaking her head. "I'm happy to do this."

"Well, I appreciate it," he replied, forcefully pulling his gaze away. Actually, he appreciated everything about her. Her kind, unselfish and giving nature most of all.

"Bye," she called, her voice soft.

"Bye." He waved over his shoulder, forcing himself not to turn around, to get on with his day as planned, thanks to Allison's unexpected yet generous offer.

She was a good friend, and he needed one of those right now, and the kids needed as many positive female role models as possible in their lives. How could he deny them that?

She'd watch the kids, he'd be grateful and he and the twins could stop by for Story Time once in a while so Nicky and Rosie could see their new favorite person. Everything would be fine, as long as he remembered his set-in-stone priorities.

Chapter Six

Two hours after Sam left the twins at Happy Endings, Allison realized she couldn't remember when she'd had a better time. She was glad she'd gone with her gut and offered to take care of them, even though Sam had clearly been reluctant to impose.

The dinner hour was typically slow, so Viv had taken over the rest of the store and Allison had hunkered down on the beanbag chairs in the Kids' Korner with Rosie and Nicky to entertain them with books. She alternated reading stories about cars and trucks with those about princesses and horses, and both kids sat quietly, cuddled up on either side of her, engaged and cooperative. Near-perfect behavior.

They really were wonderful kids, and as the afternoon had worn on, she couldn't help but wish they were hers; just the thought of being with them every day brought forth a wistful longing she couldn't suppress, as if they filled a hollow space inside her in a way nothing else could. She'd always dreamed of being a mom. Maybe someday. But not with these kids.

She had other plans, other people counting on her. She was counting on herself to focus on her own dreams. Her path was set, and she wouldn't dream of stepping off it.

After a bit, she got out some sock puppets she kept at the store for children who visited and gave into the twins' begging for a made-up story using the puppets. Soon she had them giggling with glee as they lolled on the beanbag chairs, relaxed and silly, adding their own whimsical tidbits to the story as they went along.

"Well, well," a male voice said. "What's going on back here?"

Allison's pulse leaped, but she held it together and leaned back on the edge of the beanbag so her head hung over the side, backward. An upside-down Sam stood there, holding food bags. Viv, who was still here, must have let him in.

"We're making up stories," Allison replied. Was it seven already? My, how time flew when she was having a great time.

Nicky jumped up. "Miss Allison has these socks puppies!"

"Yeah," Rosie exclaimed. "We're pretending they're dragons!"

"Well, that sounds like a lot of fun." Sam moved closer. Even upside down he looked fantastic, athletic yet put together. "Anyone hungry for burgers and fries?"

"I am," Rosie said, standing. "Yum."

"Me, too," Nicky added, running over to his dad. "I love fries."

Allison clambered from the floor and the aroma of the food hit her full force. "Wow, that smells good." Better she smell food rather than Sam's spicy aftershave.

"I'm hungry, too." He set the bags down on

the kid-size table in the center of the Kids' Korner. "But first we have to go wash our hands."

"Good suggestion," Allison added, liking being part of a team with Sam.

They all traipsed back to the restrooms and took turns washing up, and then the kids and Sam headed back to the Kids' Korner to eat while Allison went to her office at the back of the store and grabbed some paper plates, napkins and bottles of water from the minifridge she kept there for the lunches she usually ate in, along with the blanket she'd brought from home for when the weather turned cold and her office might get drafty.

When she got back to the Kids' Korner, the twins had the sock puppets on their hands and were singing some kind of song as they moved the puppets' mouths.

Sam gave her a bemused look. "I guess socks are fun."

"I guess so." Allison held the blanket up. "Who wants to have a picnic?"

"Me!" the twins answered together.

"Well, then, come on over and help me spread this blanket out on the floor."

They did as asked—Allison commented on what good little helpers they were—and soon they had a nice little burger picnic set up. Everyone sat in a circle, boy, girl, boy, girl, and when they were settled, Sam handed out the food and dumped the fries into the bag to share.

Something occurred to Allison, and she got to her feet. "I'll be right back." She headed out to the front counter to talk to Viv, who was closing out register two. "Hey, you," Allison said.

"Hey back."

"Listen, we're having burgers and fries back there. You want to join us?" She wouldn't feel right excluding Viv.

Viv smiled. "Thanks, but no. I have to get home and feed the fur babies." Viv was single and had a hamster named Roger, for Roger Bannister and his four-minute mile, and a cat named Esmeralda, Essie for short.

"You sure?"

"Positive." She pointed toward the Kids'

Korner. "You better get back there and eat your dinner. Sam and the kids are waiting."

Sam and the kids are waiting. The sound of that made Allison's heart warm. But she couldn't let her heart rule her head. Not with so much at stake. "Okay. I'll see you tomorrow."

As Viv had predicted, Sam and the kids sat, waiting for her to eat.

"Sorry about that." She lowered herself to the floor and her knee touched Sam's. She swallowed and tried to act normal. "I asked Viv to join us, but she has to get home."

Sam nodded. "That was nice of you."

"The more the merrier," Allison said. And the safer? Probably. Too late now.

Sam grabbed a fry. "Who can find the longest one?"

Giggling, the kids held up a fry, and Allison did, too.

"Nicky wins," Sam said.

Between bites of burger they continued that game, and periodically Allison peeked at Sam, not quite able to believe the boy she'd loved from afar was here with her, along with his two adorable children.

Filled with equal parts happiness and gut-munching apprehension that set her on an uneasy edge, her appetite faded and everything she ate tasted like sawdust.

"You not hungry?" Sam asked, nudging her knee.

She looked at him, noticing the dark flecks in his eyes. "Um…I had a muffin from Sweet Dreams Bakery this afternoon, and I guess it stuck with me."

True enough. It wasn't as if she could say, "Not really, because you being here, touching my knee, has got me so flipped out I can't eat." Put that way, she felt like a silly girl with a crush, and that was the last thing she wanted.

"Lori said that place is really good."

"It is." Sweet Dreams was another Save Our Street business, and was run by Melissa Sweeney. She was now engaged to Brian Montclair, whom she'd hired to help out at the bakery. They'd fallen in love and were planning a January wedding. "Of course, I do have a bit of a sweet tooth, so I'm partial."

"I'll have to give it a try."

His mention of Lori brought up a thought. "So, what's Lori up to?" Allison tried another fry and it tasted delicious. Maybe the change in subject was a good thing for her appetite.

"Haven't you talked to her?"

A bit of shame marched through Allison; she'd felt bad she hadn't made the first move when she arrived in Bygones and contacted Lori. "Um…no. I've been really busy getting the store open and off the ground." True enough. She'd been working insane hours since she'd arrived in Bygones. "I didn't hear from her, and I didn't make the first move."

Sam rested his forearms on his knees. "Yeah, not surprising now that I think about it. She and Joe were gone for the past two months on a cross-country driving trip to see his family in Oregon. They just got back last week."

She shrugged. "I have to admit, our friendship fell off our senior year in high school, and I always had the impression she was mad at me or something."

He frowned. "Mad at you?"

"Yeah, it seemed like she was avoiding me."

"That's odd."

"I thought so, too." Allison took a bite of burger. "I tend to be sensitive when it comes to stuff like that, though, so maybe I imagined it." Her parents' emotional neglect had produced some pretty deep insecurities, and in certain instances, oversensitivity. She did her best to modulate being easily upset, but sometimes her lack of self-confidence got the best of her and she read things that weren't there into situations.

"You're sensitive?" Sam asked.

"Sometimes." Often, actually. She just had a lot or practice hiding it. "Does that surprise you?"

"Actually, it does. You seem very levelheaded and grounded to me." His eyes searched her face. "Not too sensitive at all."

His praise—and visual perusal—set off sparklers inside her and her face heated. She looked down and swirled a fry in some ketchup, hoping he didn't see her blush. "Well, thanks."

"I'm sure Lori would love to hear from you."

"She has two kids, right?"

"Right. Jacob is four and Katy is three."

"A girl and a boy." Just what Allison had always wanted—a daughter to share girlie stuff with and a rough-and-tumble boy to horse around with, though girls liked horsing around, too. Her sisters could run circles around just about anybody on the basketball court.

Rosie and Nicky were quietly eating, so Allison decided to take advantage of their being occupied and kept the conversation with Sam going. "Your dad must be thrilled with all his grandkids." Allison's parents had never even mentioned any desire for grandkids. Not that she saw them that often, but still…

"Yeah, he dotes on them."

She envied that; if history proved true, her own parents wouldn't have time for any of their future grandkids. But, boy, would they have a successful wheat farm. Talk about messed-up priorities, something she wouldn't repeat with her own kids when she had them someday. She would work hard now, when she didn't have children, and hopefully be established enough when she did to shower them with attention.

"I always thought your dad was the nicest man. He took me and Lori fishing pretty often." Allison had always wished Sam would join them, but he was busy with sports and his girlfriend and never had time.

"He's a good guy, and he still loves to fish."

Allison nibbled on the last part of her bun. "Did he ever remarry?"

Sam shook his head as he took a drink of water. "Nope. He's never even dated anyone. My mom's abandonment pretty much ruined love for him."

"Oh, wow. That's sad." The Franklin family had never been the same since Mrs. Franklin took off, never to return. She didn't even keep in touch.

"You think?" Sam popped the last bite of burger into his mouth.

She furrowed her brow. "Yes. Don't you?"

"Well, from a strictly emotional point of view, yes, it's a bit sad that he doesn't believe in love. But from a pragmatic standpoint, I think it makes sense."

She couldn't believe what she was hearing; Sam had always had plenty of girlfriends and had seemed gung-ho on finding love in high school. Plus, he'd married right out of college. Had he changed that much? Of course, he *had* been through a devastating divorce. "I didn't take you for such a cynic."

"I didn't used to be." He lowered his voice. "But now… Well, now I know better than to put much stock in love."

"So you're never going to fall in love again?" Allison asked, unable to keep her curiosity from taking over.

"Probably not."

Okay, wow—

Rosie let out a squawk. "No, no, Nicky, *my* fries."

"I want more," Nicky whined, trying to nab a few of the fries Rosie had put on her plate next to her burger. "You have too many."

"My food!" Rosie screeched, jerking her plate away.

"I want more fries," Nicky wailed. Big tears formed in his eyes.

"Here, Nicky, you can have the rest of mine," Allison said, moving the fries on her plate to his. "I'm done."

Sam gave Allison a grateful look. "Thank you."

"I have lots of fries now," Nicky said to Rosie. He held up his plate. "See, Ro-ro?"

Rosie shoved out her bottom lip. "I want more."

Sam put the remainder of his fries on Rosie's plate. "This is the last of them, so that's it." On a heavy breath, he ran a hand through his hair. "Okay, well, it looks like the troops are getting restless." He looked at his watch. "Oh, wow. It's seven-thirty and we've all had a long day. We need to get home." He mouthed the word *bedtime* to Allison.

They finished eating and then cleaned up, but the kids were clearly beat.

Rosie rubbed her eyes. "I'm tired, Daddy."

"Me, too." Nicky held up his arms. "You carry me, Daddy."

"All right." Sam picked Nicky up and held him high on his right side. "Although you're kinda heavy after all those fries."

"You want me to carry you?" Allison asked Rosie.

"Okay," Rosie said. "Piggyback?"

Allison held out her arms. "Let's stick with regular carrying right now, all right?"

"'Kay," Rosie said as Allison lifted her. Rosie put her arms around Allison's neck and laid her head down on her shoulder. "You smell nice, Miss Allison."

"Well, thank you, Rosie." Rosie's hug felt wonderful, all warm and cozy, and once again, Allison felt a pang that these kids weren't hers. They would always hold a special place in her heart, though. She'd make sure of it.

Sam led the way through the store and out the door to his SUV. Allison followed, murmuring under her breath to Rosie, and heard Sam softly talking to Nicky. The situation had a warm contentedness enveloping

Allison like a fuzzy blanket, and she wondered why.

Then it hit her; it was such a simple thing, the act of carrying a sleepy kid to the car with another adult, but the actions seemed so intimate, so…bonding.

Sam unlocked the car, his dark head bent, his arms holding Nicky close, and sharp longing hit her full force, right in the heart, taking her breath away. This is what it would be like if she and Sam were a couple. A team.

Allison almost dropped Rosie. Whoa. Slow down. She could not let her warm fuzzy thoughts take over. Sure, Sam had been her Prince Charming in high school. But that was then and this was now, and she certainly wasn't that idealistic girl anymore. She was a no-nonsense businesswoman, and her focus was on Happy Endings, on making herself a success, on proving herself after ten years of flitting from this to that.

She had to remember what she wanted in her life right now. And it couldn't be Sam and the twins as anything other than friends. That was what he wanted, too. All the more reason to keep her attention where it belonged and her heart safely tucked away.

Both kids had conked out by the time Sam had the SUV in the garage, so he coaxed them from their car seats and carried them into the dark house at the same time, one in each arm. Moving efficiently, he headed straight for the room they shared upstairs next to the master bedroom.

He laid them down and then made quick work of getting them into their pajamas. Within minutes they were tucked into their twin beds, both surrounded by their favorite stuffed animals.

He bent and kissed Nicky's head. "Good night, buddy. I love you."

Nicky just snuffled and turned over.

Sam moved to Rosie's bed and bent and kissed her forehead. "Night-night, Rosie-roo."

She threw her arms around his neck. "Night-night, Daddy." A pause. "Are we going to go see Miss Allison tomorrow?"

He sat on the edge of the bed. "Um…there's no Story Time tomorrow, so probably not."

Mild disappointment moved through him and he frowned inwardly. What was that all about?

"Maybe we can go and play with the socks puppies." Rosie held up a hand and moved her fingers as if she had a puppet.

"Miss Allison owns the bookstore, and she has to work." And so did he. Which reminded him, he still needed to find someone to watch the twins tomorrow. Great.

"But she likes us, and we like her, so we can go see her all the time, right?"

Her child's logic made him smile. "Well, sure, mostly. But she has to work, so we can't expect her to drop everything to play with you guys, right?"

"So she should come over here," Rosie said on a yawn. "And bring the socks puppies with her."

Sam wasn't sure that was a good idea, but he didn't exactly want to get into a discussion with Rosie about his reasons, so he just said, "We'll see." The kids were still too young to know that that answer meant he was hedging.

"Okay, Daddy," she said, turning over. "I'm going to sleep right now."

He rose. "Okay, I'll see you in the morning. I love you."

"Love you, too."

He left the room, making sure the nightlight was on, and then headed downstairs. The house was dark and seemed chilled, so he went to the thermostat and pressed Warm twice. Operating on autopilot, he went into the kitchen, turned on a light and got a drink of water while he stood looking out the window over the sink. The sun had set and the yard was dark, and he was sure he'd hear the leaves rustling in the wind if he went out back. Fall was coming and the holidays weren't far behind.

All at once a sense of hollow loneliness swept through him like a cold wind, making the space under his breastbone ache. A lot of the time while he was at home, he had no one to talk to, no one to sit on the couch with. No one to hold. And he had his empty bed waiting when he turned in. He grimaced.

He was lonely. What single parent wasn't?

His thoughts swung to Allison. When he'd walked into the Kids' Korner and seen her on those beanbag chairs with the twins, reading stories, well, something warm and fuzzy had dissolved inside him. And when she'd helped him carry the twins to the car? Man, it had felt good to have someone helping him. Maybe that's what had him feeling so melancholy; her being part of his "team" would be brief. No way around that.

Whatever the case, he had to stop letting glimpses of an impossible life get to him. What good would that do, except to drive him nuts? So the kids could spend time with Allison—he wouldn't deprive them of that—but he had to keep himself personally detached.

He finished his water, washed the glass and set it on the drain board. Time to find some day care for tomorrow. Maybe Dad was feeling better and could help him out. He picked up the phone and called.

Ten minutes later Sam had had part of his problem solved—Dad could watch the kids during the day, but had a commitment in the late afternoon and couldn't help out during practice.

Dad confirmed that Lori was still out of town, so Sam called the neighbor girl, Shawna, on the off chance that she'd be available. No go; she had a PSAT study class after school, which he realized many of the younger teenagers around were probably attending, though not the members of his team because they were all juniors and seniors.

Great. He was back in the same spot he'd been in today—needing a sitter during practice. He shook his head and muttered under his breath, "Thanks a lot, Teresa." His thoughts came around to Allison again. He tapped his fingers on the counter. Calling her and asking for another favor just didn't sit right with him, though she'd said she'd help out anytime, and he believed her. That was the kind of gal she was, giving and helpful.

But it wasn't as if he had a lot of other options; it wasn't fair to cancel practice because his ex-wife was an undependable flake. So he'd call Allison in the morning and hope she could help out. The kids would be thrilled if she agreed. And he'd be nothing more than grateful.

Chapter Seven

The next morning, Allison had already been at work for two hours when the phone rang. "Happy Endings Bookstore. This is Allison. How may I help you?"

"Hey, Allison, it's Sam."

Her tummy went all pretzely. "Oh, um, Sam." She cleared her throat and tightened her grip on the phone handset. "Hi. What's up?"

He paused. "Listen, I'm in a bind again, and I hate to ask, but is your offer to watch the twins during practice today still open?"

"Of course it is." No chore there; she loved spending time with Rosie and Nicky.

"Well, great. My dad's watching them today

while I'm at work, so is it okay if I bring them by at about four-thirty?"

"That'll be fine." Then she remembered something. "I'm having my first creative-writing workshop for teens at three-thirty, but we should be wrapping up by four-thirty or so."

"Oh, yeah, I remember you told me about those." He paused, then said, "I think I mentioned that some of the guys on the team might benefit from that kind of class. One kid in particular."

"Well, tell them there's pizza afterward, and teenage girls will be in attendance, too. My sister Amy is coming and bringing some of her friends."

He chuckled. "Girls and pizza. Sounds like you've got their number."

"Not me, Amy. She thought of it because she's boy crazy and wanted to make things more fun for her and her friends. I agreed because it'll bring in more participants."

"Hard to believe we were ever that age, isn't it?"

"They do seem really young."

"And carefree. No responsibilities."

"True." Although as a teen Allison had always been responsible for her younger siblings while her parents worked.

"Well, thanks, I owe you. In fact, I owe you twice."

"You don't owe me anything."

"Oh, yes, I do, and I intend to pay you back." A moment's silence filled the line. "In fact, why don't you just let me actually pay you for watching the twins. I can't believe I didn't think of that before."

She shook her head. "Absolutely not, Sam. We're friends, and friends help friends."

"I owe you, Allison, and I won't ever forget that. If you ever need a favor, just ask."

Something occurred to her. "Well, since you mentioned it…"

"What?" he said.

She held back, not sure she should actually ask Sam for help.

"Do you need a favor or something?" he asked. "Because if you do, please just ask. I'll feel better if I can repay you in some way for all your help with the twins."

"Okay. One of the things the kids from the writing workshop are going to do is man a literacy booth at the harvest festival a week from Saturday. I could use some help with the actual building of the booth sometime between now and then."

"Just name the place and time, and I'm your man," Sam replied. "I even have the tools."

Her man. Her tummy fell. "Um...actually, what I really need is your muscles," she said, then realized the implications of her statement. "I mean...what I meant to say is, I need your, um, strength. You know, for the lifting and stuff." Talk about a blubbering idiot. What was she, twelve?

He laughed. "I knew what you meant, and my muscles are perfectly willing to do any heavy lifting. It's the least I can do."

They said goodbye and Allison hung up. She rubbed her damp hand on her pant leg and wondered if she were crazy to ask Sam to help with the literacy booth. Well, at least this way they'd be even, and he wouldn't feel indebted to her.

Why didn't that make her feel any better?

* * *

Allison opened the door to Happy Endings. Sam and two very tall teenage boys stood there on the sidewalk, the same two young men whom she'd seen talking to Sam at the Everything the other night. They all wore sweats and huge basketball shoes. But Sam was the only one who made her heartbeat go funky.

"Hey, guys," she said, sounding normal, thank goodness. "Glad you could stop by." She waved them in.

Sam made the introductions. "Rory and Scott, this is the bookstore's owner, Allison True."

"Nice to meet you, ma'am," they both said.

She closed the door and turned, and then looked up—way up. "Wow, you boys are tall." Her gaze bounced to Sam. "Even taller than you."

"Yeah, we get that a lot," Rory said.

"Rory is the starting center on the team," Sam added.

"What do your parents feed you?" she asked.

"Anything, as long as there's lots of it," Scott replied, swiping his longish blond hair out of his face. He wasn't quite as tall as Sam but was to her untrained eye a bit huskier.

"I remember those days." Sam shook his head. "I was a literal bottomless pit when I was these guys' age."

"I do seem to recall you ate a lot," Allison remarked. "And I also remember your dad was quite a good cook."

"He still is."

"Did you really know Coach when he was our age?" Rory asked.

"You bet I did." She'd wished desperately back then to know him even better.

Scott leaned in with a grin. "What was he like?"

She blinked. "Um, well…he was popular, and a great basketball player—the star center, actually, just like you, Rory. And he was a nice guy, too." He had never been a mean older brother and had never teased or tormented Lori. In fact, Allison recalled that he'd been pretty protective of his sister and had made it clear that he had her back. Allison had always liked that about him.

"Did he have a girlfriend?" Rory snickered, and then nudged Scott.

Yes. And it hadn't been Allison, much to her disappointment. "Pretty sure he did," she said vaguely, thinking they'd think it was weird if she rattled off a name right off the top of her head. "I seem to remember she was the head cheerleader." Actually, she remembered everything about Kristy Wainright—she'd been blond, pretty, bubbly and the girl every guy at Bygones High wanted to date. And the girl nerdy little Allison had desperately wanted to be.

Sam shot her a desperate look. "Yes, she was."

"How long did you guys date?" Scott asked Sam.

"Most of our senior year, until I went off to college."

The way Allison had heard the story, Kristy, a junior, had been devastated when Sam broke it off before he'd left for school, but not for long. She'd gotten pregnant her senior year, dropped out and married the father, then divorced him five years and two more kids later. As far as Allison knew, she'd moved away and no longer lived in Bygones.

"I'd like to date the head cheerleader," Rory said. "But she doesn't even know I exist."

Allison knew that feeling. Sam hadn't been aware of her as anything but Lori's friend, either. She opened her mouth to respond, then noticed Sam giving her a significant look, as if to say, "Rescue me." Obviously he wasn't comfortable with the subject matter.

Cluing in, she crooked a finger over her shoulder. "Hey, guys. Some of the other kids are still here, and there's still plenty of pizza left, so go on through and I'll be back in a bit to talk to you two about the workshop, all right?"

"Great, I'm starving," Rory said, rubbing his hands together. "Pizza sounds good."

"Yeah, me, too," Scott said, adjusting his backpack. "I could eat a horse right about now."

"Well, go on and have at it," Allison said.

"And tell Amy that I'll be back in a minute and take the twins off her hands."

Sam held back. "Let's hold back for a few minutes and let them socialize a bit before we swoop in with talk of creative writing."

"Good idea." Allison looked at Sam. "Guess we got off track a little there."

"No big deal. I just feel funny talking about my dating history with the boys."

"Understood." She should have figured that out sooner. "But no surprise they were interested, seeing as how we're ancient to them. As far as they're concerned, we have one foot in the grave at this point."

"No kidding. I had to work a little harder to block shots at practice today," he said ruefully, shaking his head. "I got schooled by a bunch of teenagers."

"Oh, I doubt that." She waved a hand in the air. "You had mad court skills back in high school."

Sam's brows went up. "You remember that?"

Oh, yes. She recalled everything about him. "I went to all the games." Because he was playing, though she wouldn't tell him that. "With Lori," she belatedly added.

"Oh, okay." He grinned. "I thought maybe you went just to watch me."

Obviously he was teasing. But this comment was completely accurate. "Yeah, that was it," she teased back. What better way to deflect the truth than to throw his joke back at him? "I just had to see number twenty-two in action."

"You remember my number, too?"

Whoopsie. "I...guess I do," she retorted, trying to sound casual, even though that number was branded in her brain; she'd once covered an entire page of notebook paper in 22s during a particularly boring math class. Yeah, she'd had it bad for Sam Franklin. That thought had her moving toward the front counter.

Sam followed. "Wow. You've got some memory."

Suddenly it seemed a bit silly to be skirting the truth about something that happened when they were teenagers. That was long past and had no relevance now. Plus, it bordered on deceitful, and that wasn't her intention.

"Well, I may have had some…admiration for you." She felt her face heat, so she looked away, pretending to peruse some paperwork; who would have guessed she would ever share that secret with him?

"Really?"

"Really." She looked at him, noting his slack jaw. He seemed genuinely surprised by her statement. "You were the star basketball player. Every girl at Bygones High had a crush on you," she said to minimize the depth of her own feelings just a bit. Though what was past was past.

"Wow. I had no idea."

"Not surprising. You never had a big head." That was always one of the things she'd loved about him—his lack of an ego was very appealing. It still was.

"Yeah, my dad would never have stood for that," he replied. "He's one of the most down-to-earth, humble people I've ever known."

"I remember." Allison straightened the business-card holder on the counter. "Didn't he make you and Lori contribute a portion of your allowances to charity every month?"

"Yep. I used to hate that, but now I appreciate it." He unzipped his jacket. "In fact, I'm going to do that with the twins when they're old enough to understand the concept."

"You had a good role model, didn't you?"

"The best."

"You're lucky. Not everybody has that." Like her. Her dad had always been focused on the business rather than his kids. Unfortunately, her mom had the same mind-set, so there were zero good-parenting role models in her life.

He studied her. "I get the feeling you speak from personal experience."

She swallowed. Oh, boy. But…she was being honest here. Would it hurt to open up just a bit, even though she usually opted not to share how dysfunctional the True family was? She'd always been so ashamed that she and her sisters hadn't come first with their parents. But who better to understand her family issues than Sam, whose mom had taken off and never been seen since? He could probably empathize…

"Actually, I do. My parents weren't the best role models in the world."

Sam leaned on the counter, his eyes soft. Disarming. Yet compelling, too. "How so?"

Before she could shove out a response, Nicky came bounding up. "Hi, Daddy!" he exclaimed. "You are here."

Sam turned and scooped Nicky up into his arms and gave him a big hug. "Yes, I'm back. Did you have fun with Miss Allison?"

"Yes." Nicky nodded. "And Miss Amy, too. We had pizza with sprinkles on the top." In other words, Parmesan cheese.

"I know. Is there any left for me?" Sam asked. "Or did you eat it all?"

"Prolly." Nicky pointed to the back of the store. "Want to go see?"

"You bet I do." Sam turned and looked at Allison. "Can we finish our discussion another time?"

"Of course," she replied. "Go eat and I'll be there in a few minutes to talk about the workshop to Scott and Rory."

"Great." He turned his attention to Nicky. "Let's go look into pizza, okay, bud?" Still holding Nicky, Sam headed toward the Kids' Korner.

Allison watched him go, letting out a belated sigh. Of relief, she realized. Hmm. Revealing. In theory, opening up to Sam about her family seemed doable. Maybe even good for her, in that talking sometimes helped her deal. But was Sam the right person to confide in? She hoped she could figure out the answer to that question before it was too late to turn back.

As Sam headed back to the Kids' Korner, he thought about what Allison had told him.

She'd had a crush on him? Amazing. He'd never suspected. If he had, he would have asked her out for sure, no matter what Lori had done to discourage him. Even now, Allison's revelation had his stomach doing jumping jacks. But…a lot had happened since his carefree days of high school. He was different now, wiser, toughened up. He had kids and job problems and a manipulative ex-wife to handle. Enough family drama for many years to come. He couldn't let Allison's confession matter, or lower his guard.

He found Rosie and the teens in the Kids' Korner eating pizza as they lounged on multicolored beanbag chairs. Amy True, whom he recognized from school, had Rosie on her lap and was reading her a story. He could definitely see her resemblance to Allison; she had the same blue eyes and brown hair. The other girl, Tiffany Preston, a petite blonde, was texting on her cell phone. The pizza sat on a table in the corner, along with some bottles of water.

"Coach!" Rory lifted a slice of pizza. "You hungry?"

Sam put Nicky down and eyed the chow. "I could eat."

"Daddy, Miss Amy is reading me a story," Rosie said. "About a princess."

Amy waved. "Hey, Mr. Franklin."

He returned the wave as he headed over to the pizza and picked up a slice. "Amy, Tiffany. You girls keeping these boys in line?"

"Actually, Rosie here is doing that for us." Amy high-fived Rosie. "You go, girl."

"Yeah, Ro-ro, you go," Nicky mimicked, plopping down in a beanbag chair next to Scott.

Allison returned to the Kids' Korner. "Welcome, Scott and Rory. I've already laid out the parameters of the class for the other kids, but I'll go over things while you eat, if you don't mind."

"Please do," Sam said. He was looking forward to seeing her in her element.

"So, boys," she said, "I already talked to the girls, and the other kids who were here earlier, about their goals for the workshop. Why are you here?"

"For the pizza," Scott said, licking his fingers.

"Yeah, eating's my goal," Rory added.

"Well, that's a given." Allison picked up a napkin and handed it to Scott. "What I meant was, what do you hope to accomplish? I'm perfectly willing to tailor the class to help in any way I can."

Sam piped up, "Writing in general would

help a lot." He knew from talking to Sharon Wells, the boys' English teacher, that both of them were struggling with the essay assignments.

"Yeah, I'm bad at it," Rory said. "My grade in English is, like, awful."

"Me, too," Tiffany said. "Grammar is not my friend."

"Okay, I can work with that." Allison looked at Scott and Rory. "The assignment for today is to write a personal-experience piece about your favorite thing and how it's impacted your life."

"Oh, man." Rory rolled his eyes. "We have assignments?"

"I know, what a drag, huh?" Tiffany said, her eyes on her cell phone.

"Tiffany, remember the rule we have about phones?" Allison gave her a pointed look.

Tiffany looked up, then grudgingly put her phone down. "Yeah."

"Thank you." Allison went on, "Do you guys want to improve and pass your English class, or not?" She looked right at Rory, and then shifted her focus to Scott. "Won't you two lose your spots on the team if your GPA isn't good?"

Sam wanted to chime in with the answer but kept quiet, preferring to let the boys tell their own story. "Well, yeah," Rory said, shrugging. "Not to mention my dad will freak if I fail English."

"Well, then, there you go," Allison said. "All the more reason to take advantage of this class. The format of the workshop is to do the assignment, and then we'll discuss what you wrote at the next class and offer feedback."

"So I have to read my stuff out loud?" Scott looked horrified.

"Yes, but everyone will do it, and we only allow constructive criticism, so it should be a very good way to learn."

Sam liked the idea. Peer feedback was always helpful; teens often took more stock in what other teens had to say than they did in the opinions of adults.

"Actually, I have a suggestion," Amy said.

"Go ahead," Allison replied.

"How about we all write a skit together to

do at the harvest festival when we man the literacy booth?"

"That's a great idea," Allison said. "Would you boys be up for that?"

"Do we get to work with them?" Rory asked, nodding toward Amy and Tiffany.

"Yep, you do," Allison said. "You'd write the skit together, man the booth and perform the skit with them."

"Then I'm in," Rory said.

Scott raised a hand. "Me, too."

"You girls up for this?"

Both girls nodded.

"Great!" Allison grinned. "This'll be fun."

Rory held up his hand. "Yo, Ms. True. Does writing the skit count as our assignment for this week?"

Sam's teacher's sense had seen this question coming.

Allison paused, clearly mulling over her answer. She looked to Sam. "What do you think, Mr. Franklin?"

"I think it should count, especially since there's a skit involved." He gave Scott and

Rory a skeptical glance. "I only hope you guys are better at acting than I am."

Allison chuckled. "Don't worry, boys, no one expects good acting. It's the message being delivered that matters."

"Good thing," Scott said, nudging Rory with his foot. "Though I'm better at acting than this guy."

Rory snorted. "No way, dude."

"So," Allison remarked, "I'm going to leave it up to you guys to get together before next week to write the script, and then you can show me what you've got then, all right?"

All the teens agreed.

"Great," Allison said. "Why don't you talk amongst yourselves and come up with the core idea for the skit, and then run it by me and Mr. Franklin before you leave. I'll contact the other kids who've already left and let them know what's going on."

The teens put their heads together, and, surprisingly, Nicky in particular was content to sit still in his beanbag, "reading" his book, though his gaze kept darting to the older boys.

Sam took the opportunity to snag another piece of pizza, covertly watching Allison as she bent down and said something to Rosie. Rosie nodded, and then Allison picked her up and came over to Sam.

"We're going to go wash our hands," Allison said, holding out one of Rosie's hands, which had smears of pizza sauce on them.

"I'll take her," he said.

"I want Miss Allison to take me," Rosie said. "Please?"

"Do you mind?" he asked Allison.

"Of course not." Allison rubbed a finger on Rosie's cheek. "I think we may have to wash your face, too, Miss Rosie-roo. I see a little stray sauce there."

Allison left the Kids' Korner with Rosie propped on her hip. Just before they disappeared around a bookshelf, Allison whispered in Rosie's ear. Rosie giggled and whispered back.

Something in the vicinity of Sam's chest softened, sending tendrils of warmth outward. Nicky asked him to come look at a picture of a sports car in the book he was reading and Sam hunkered down next to him, grateful for the distraction.

A few minutes later, Allison came back with a spotlessly clean Rosie. The older kids wrapped up their discussion and presented their skit idea, which he and Allison approved. Then all the teens left together with talk of getting ice cream at the Everything on their way home.

Allison pushed the door closed after them. "Whew. It's been a long day."

"You've been busy, haven't you?"

"Yes, but I love what I do, so I don't mind," she said with a smile. "It's way better than working my fingers to the bone for the Book Barn. This place is mine, and that makes all the difference."

"You're really determined to make the most out of this store, aren't you?"

"Yes, I am." She lifted her chin.

"I admire your commitment." He paused, then added, "You really have a knack with those kids."

"Well, thanks again." She turned and

headed back to the Kids' Korner. "I enjoy spending time with them."

He followed her. "High school kids are a tough crowd. You really know how to talk to them."

She looked over her shoulder. "I remember what it was like being that age, so I try to tap into that and make things interesting for them."

"They seem very interested in helping out with the literacy booth."

She stopped when they reached the Kids' Korner. "Speaking of that, are you still up for helping build the booth?" she asked, her gorgeous blue eyes hitting him straight on. "I'm a mess with power tools."

He paused. He had promised, hadn't he? And he wasn't one to go back on his promises.

She went on, "I've decided to ask the teens to help out, and that we'll just build the booth in the church basement so we don't have to move it there before the festival."

So the kids would be there. Good. He

rubbed his cheek. "I'm fine with that," Sam said. "Just tell me when and I'm there."

Allison's mouth curved up into a lovely smile. "Wonderful. It'll be fun. I was thinking Friday night after the store closes so Viv can help, if that works for you. We can make a party out of it with the kids."

"That works," he said. It would be a group activity, with the teens present, and Viv, too. Nothing more than him helping out where needed. Though he didn't even want to think about why that even mattered.

Some things were best left as mysteries.

Chapter Eight

Allison looked at the pile of wood Sam had deposited in the basement of Bygones Community Church. "Thanks for bringing this here. It never would have fit into my car." He'd picked up the wood she'd ordered from the Fixer-Upper, and she was beyond grateful for his help with the heavy lifting and hauling.

"Glad I could make use of my truck." He gestured to Scott and Rory. "Luckily I had these two guys to help."

Rory flexed his skinny arms. "Yeah, Coach didn't do anything. It was all us, Ms. True."

Scott snorted. "Not with those arms, dude."

He flexed, too, cartoon style. "Now, these are some guns."

Allison chuckled. "Well, either way, I appreciate the help." She looked up and saw Amy and Tiffany come in. "Ah, here are the girls." Each girl carried a shopping bag full of treats to be eaten with dinner after the booth was complete.

"When's dinner?" Scott asked.

Did these boys think about anything but food? "I brought sandwiches and chips, and I made cookies and brought some candy, but we have to work first," Allison said. "There's water over there in the blue cooler."

Viv came in, her arms loaded down with the banner she'd made with the help of the electronic cutting machine her mother owned and the literature she had printed at Happy Endings. She was quite good with designing stuff on the computer. "I finally finished this banner," she said. "Good thing my mom knows how to operate that machine, or I never would have gotten it made."

"Here, Viv, let me help you with that." Sam, gentleman that he was, went over and took the banner off her hands, along with some of the flyers.

"Thanks," Viv said.

"No problem," Sam replied, carefully placing the bright red paper banner on the floor in the corner.

Allison clapped her hands. "All right, everyone is here." She pulled out some papers she'd folded and put in the back pocket of her jeans. "Here are the plans for the booth."

Sam blinked. "Did you draw those yourself?"

"No, I did not." She could expound books and literature from sunup to sundown, but design plans were not in her wheelhouse. "I got them off the internet."

"Resourceful." Sam grinned. "I like that."

"I try," she said. "I only hope your mathematical acumen comes in handy when you try to figure out the cut angles and such." Plus, she was counting on him for the power-tool operation; her experience was limited to a one-time workshop at the Fixer-Upper, and she didn't feel confident in her abilities. Maybe she could handle some of the nailing.

"I think I can do that," he said, coming closer, holding out his hand. "Mind if I take a look?"

"Sure." She handed him the plans and his fingers touched hers briefly. Sparks flew up her arm and it was all she could do not to gasp out loud.

Seemingly unaffected, Sam looked over the plans, his brow creased. "These look pretty straightforward." He glanced up at the teens. "Actually, I might find a way to give you guys some math credit for this project."

"Cool," Rory said. The other teens nodded in agreement.

Sam handed the plans back to Allison, and then went over and put on the tool belt he'd brought, slinging the leather job low on his hips. Allison made a concerted effort not to stare, but really, was there anything more attractive than a man in a tool belt? Unfortunately not. She was going to need to focus on the project, not Sam, no matter how good he looked in his craftsman persona.

After some discussion about how to proceed, and some rough division of labor, the group got to work. Sam supervised the board measuring and cutting as per the plans, and soon they moved on to nailing the pieces together. Allison could see the teacher in Sam shine through; he was very patient with the kids and took time to explain the building process in a way that made the project fun yet educational.

She found her gaze snagging on him often as he helped one teen or another with the detail work of putting the booth together. Something about his demeanor really struck a chord with her. And it was much more than just how manly he looked in the tool belt. He just had a way with the teens that impressed her to no end. He was a great guy. It was such a shame he had shut himself off to the possibility of love. He could make some woman very happy someday.

A pang darted through her, but she tried to ignore it. No sense in dwelling on impossibilities.

After an hour of work, they took a dinner break—her cookies were a big hit—and then got back to work. The booth had taken shape with Sam's guidance, and soon it was time to tilt it up off the floor into an upright position. Everybody pitched in, and Allison ended up next to Sam, bent down close as they worked to get hold of the framework that formed the booth.

As they worked to lift the booth, he turned and flashed a quick smile, and her heart leaped. Then his large hand touched hers, his firm shoulder pressed against her arm and his hip jostled hers. He was warm and solid and she didn't pull away, though she probably should have, except there really wasn't room for her to move away with Viv on Allison's other side. So she let herself enjoy the brief contact, telling herself touching him was just part of the job.

All too soon the booth was upright and the moment had passed. Allison did her best to act normal, though her gaze seemed to follow Sam wherever he went.

Viv brought the banner over. "Let's see how this thing is gonna look."

"Good idea." Allison needed a distraction from watching Sam anyway. Anything would

do. "I'll hold this end and you hold the other."
She stretched to hold the banner up in its spot
over the booth. Except she wasn't tall enough
to really hold it in the right place. Neither was
Viv, so the banner just sagged in the middle.

Sam came over. "Here, let me." He took
the end of the banner from Allison and she
stepped back, careful not to touch him. "Rory,
you're tall. Take Ms. Duncan's end and let's
really see how this is going to look."

Rory did as instructed, and soon the banner
was stretched out in its proper place. It read,
Reading and Writing is Fun in bright yellow
block lettering. The Happy Endings loaded-
bookshelf logo, printed in full color, graced
the middle of the banner under the writing.

"Oh, my," Allison breathed. "It's perfect."
Seeing her own bookstore's logo never failed
to make her feel so proud she could just burst,
and so very fortunate to have the opportunity
that the SOS Committee had given her. It was
moments like these that reminded her she had
to make the store work. She just had to.

"It does look great," Sam said.

"Yeah, fantastic," Rory said.

The other kids echoed his sentiment.

"Vivian, excellent job on the banner." Sam found Allison's gaze with his own. "And you, Ms. True, have made this whole thing come together." He turned to the teens. "Kids, I hope you appreciate what these ladies have done for you. They're both going above and beyond here, and you're lucky to have them take the time to make this all happen."

Allison preened inside under his praise. Suddenly, sacrificing to make Happy Endings succeed didn't seem so much like work anymore. She was doing good here and people were noticing. Including Sam. And thanks to him and the teens here tonight, and Viv, too, all Allison's hard work was now even more worthwhile.

That was a gift she would never take for granted or waste.

Sam loaded the last of the tools into his SUV and slammed the liftgate, looking up toward the dark, cloudy sky. The weather had turned while they'd been working on the booth, and a light drizzle fell and a stiff breeze blew the falling leaves around his feet. Autumn was well on its way to Bygones.

"That was a really fun evening," Allison said from where she stood by the side of the SUV, illuminated only by the muted light shining through the church's stained-glass windows. The kids had already taken off, as had Viv, who'd left a bit earlier to go home and feed her pets. Only he and Allison had remained to clean up the last vestiges of their work party.

"Yes, it was," he replied. "I always enjoy spending time with kids." Being around Allison, he realized, was an unexpected bonus.

"Obviously, since you're a teacher. That takes a special breed, as far as I'm concerned."

"But maybe not here for long." His job was in real jeopardy. Just the thought of leaving Bygones and Bygones High School filled him with an aching sense of loss.

Just then, the wind kicked up and sent more leaves swirling. He looked skyward again. "Looks like maybe a storm's coming."

"I guess I'd better get going, then," Allison

said, zipping up the black coat she wore. "I still have some work to do with the inventory-control software at the store."

He frowned. "It's almost ten o'clock."

"I know." She grabbed her hair and corralled it in one hand. "But the software's been giving me problems. Even though Josh Smith, who's been helping all the businesses with computer setup, came by today and helped me get back on track, I still have a lot of data entry to do by Monday."

He looked at her. "You work really hard, don't you?"

"I have to. It's only me and Viv, and ultimately I'm the one in charge of making Happy Endings a viable business."

Admiration sifted through him. "Well, why don't you let me drive you to the store?" She'd driven over with Viv and had told him earlier that she planned on walking home. Guess she'd had a change in plans and was now going to the store. Whatever the case, he didn't want her walking even a few blocks in this weather. She'd be soaking wet before long.

As if to punctuate that thought, the wind gusted and the fine drizzle turned to actual rain.

Allison huddled down into her coat as she looked up. The end of the bright red scarf she wore danced. "All right. I'll take you up on that offer, now that the weather has really turned."

"Great." He moved sideways and opened the front passenger door for her and gestured inside. "My chariot awaits, Ms. True."

With a sweet smile she got in. "Why, thank you ever so much, Mr. Franklin."

"My pleasure," he said truthfully.

He closed her door, went around and climbed into the driver's seat. In no time he had the vehicle started up, the windshield wipers on and the heater going. No sense in being chilly, even for the short trip to Happy Endings.

Within a few moments, they were on their way down Granary Road toward Main Street. The town was quiet.

Allison turned in her seat and looked inquiringly at him. "It has to be really upsetting to think about losing your job."

His hand tightened on the steering wheel. "Yeah, it is. Sure, I can teach anywhere, but Bygones is my hometown and holds a special place in my heart. I don't want to leave, but supporting my family is the priority."

"Especially since your dad and Lori are here."

"Yeah, there's that, too. I'd hate to have to take my kids away from their grandpa, aunt and cousins."

"Well, if it helps at all, I'm doing everything I can to make sure Happy Endings does well, and I know all the other shop owners are, too. We all want the SOS plan to work."

"I know," he said, rolling to a stop at the intersection of Granary and Main. "And I'm trying to stay positive, but facts are facts, and I can't stick my head in the sand about my job. I've actually put out a few applications to other school districts that have openings for math teachers." He turned left onto a deserted Main Street. "I had an online video interview last week with one of them."

"Oh, wow." She unwound her scarf from her neck and put it on the seat beside her. "You're really covering your bases, then, aren't you?"

He slowed down as Happy Endings came up on his left, noting as he drove by that the lights were still on at Sweet Dreams Bakery. Guess Allison wasn't the only SOS shop owner burning the midnight oil. "I have to. I have kids to support. I need to be prepared in case the SOS plan goes south." He slanted a quick glance around, and then made a quick U-turn so he was headed the other way. "Not that I'm assuming it will, but it's all still up in the air."

"It's a solid plan with sound backing," she said firmly, lifting her chin. "It will work. All of us SOS shop owners are going to make sure of it."

He smiled at her determination, and then pulled up to the curb right in front of the store, which sat between Love in Bloom florist and the Fixer-Upper hardware store. "I believe you, if everyone puts in the kinds of hours you do." He put the truck in park and regarded Allison. "Does anyone know yet who the anonymous benefactor is?"

"No, his or her identity is still a mystery."

"I personally would be much more confident of the plan if I knew who was behind it."

"I would, too, but I'm choosing to have faith in the plan anyway." She looked right at him. "Sometimes faith is all we have."

"I used to think that," he replied. Back before Teresa had filleted his heart.

"But you don't anymore?" Allison asked softly, her small hands folded over her purse on her lap.

A throb started under his breastbone. "Not really. Divorce has a way of doing that to a person."

Allison paused. "She really hurt you, didn't she?"

The sound of the rain on the roof of the truck, along with the *thunk thunk* of the windshield wipers was the only sound for a few long moments. "Yeah."

"What happened, if you don't mind my asking?"

He tightened his jaw. No harm in sharing,

though he rarely talked about what had gone on with him and Teresa. "The marriage had been on the rocks for a while—she hated living in Bygones, and we'd been clashing over her wanting to move—so I knew we were in trouble. She didn't adjust well to motherhood, either. But for her to…cheat. Well, that was a low blow."

"The lowest." Allison paused. "You deserved better."

Her words of support eased the ache in his chest a bit. "I probably would have dealt with what she did better if not for the kids. She put herself before them, and that made her betrayal that much harder." He stretched his neck to ease some of the tension building there. "She's always wanted to play with the kids and do all the fun stuff, but she's never been into the down-and-dirty hard work of parenthood."

"I can't imagine what you've been through." Allison leaned closer ever so slightly and touched his hand. In the small confines of the vehicle, the scent of fresh peaches washed over him.

He swallowed and looked down at her hand on his; he wanted to take it in his and hold on. But that wouldn't be smart. "She's threatening to go for sole custody if I don't stay out of any kind of romantic relationship, believe it or not."

Allison quickly removed her hand. "You're kidding."

"I wish I was, but her threats are no joke."

"I, uh, didn't mean to imply they were." She paused, as if she was thinking over her response very carefully. "Do you think she has any ground to stand on?"

He lifted one shoulder. "My lawyer has advised me not to risk it, and I'm listening. Nothing is more important than my kids."

"Of course not," Allison hastily said. "You're a good dad, Sam. The best. Your children are very fortunate to have you." She looked away. "Not everyone is that blessed."

He studied her delicate profile, illuminated by just the dashboard lights, noting what looked like a slight stiffness in her jaw. "You sound like you speak from experience."

"I kind of do, actually," she said in a very small voice.

Her tone had his curiosity surging. "How so?"

She took a deep breath. "My parents were workaholics." She hesitated, then sighed. "My dad ran the farm and my mom handled the business end. Each day at sunup, they both left for the office in an outbuilding on the property. They came home after sundown, fell into bed and repeated the same thing the next day. Seven days a week."

He scratched his head, trying to make sense of what she was saying. "Running a farm the size of theirs had to be a lot of work…."

"Well, sure. But it went further than that," she said, an edge growing in her voice. "We had a babysitter when we were small, but once I was ten and my sisters came along, I learned early on how to get myself out the door to school in the morning without help. I learned to make peanut butter and jelly sandwiches about that same time. I came home, the babysitter left and I was pretty much in charge. When I was old enough, I made dinner and made sure everyone's homework was done. We were alone, just the three of us, almost all the time, and I was expected to be a live-in babysitter when I wasn't at school as soon as I was legally allowed to be left alone with my sisters."

He sensed more. He held out his hand—how could he not?—to offer a lifeline; this was obviously difficult for her to talk about. "Go on."

She took hold, and he felt her small, soft hand shaking in his grasp as she closed her eyes briefly, seemingly working up her courage to speak.

"It's okay. You can tell me," he said in the softest voice he had. He steeled himself for whatever she had to say, though his comfort wasn't more important than hers. He'd listen no matter what she told him.

She hit him with an anguish-filled gaze. "They weren't, um…demonstrative people. They never gave hugs, never came to my school events, not even my graduation. I never once heard either of them say they loved me. They called me as soon as they heard I was coming back to tell me that I was making a big mistake by taking on the store and that they thought I'd fail."

His breath stole away in a rush. All he could do was sit there, unable to imagine what she'd been through. Yes, his mom had left without a care for him and Lori, but Dad had always been there to dole out lots of hugs, unconditional love and tender care. No one had cheered louder at Sam's basketball games. No one had been prouder when Sam, and then two years later, Lori, had walked across the stage in the high school auditorium to accept their diplomas.

He saw Allison's shoulders sag, and he wanted to reach out and hold her. But he shouldn't. *Couldn't.* Not with things the way they stood, and who knew when his issues with Teresa would be resolved. But he knew how Allison felt, knew how a parent's love withheld could strike a wound so deep it never really healed.

So instead, he vocalized the empathy welling in him. "I know what it's like to be emotionally deserted by a parent."

She froze, and then her face softened. She turned toward him even more. "You do, don't you?"

"Unfortunately, yes." He looked out and saw the rain coming down and leaves clogging the gutter next to the curb. "My mom loved me and Lori so little she had no problem with just leaving and never coming back."

Allison sat quietly for a moment. "Well, we have a lot in common, then, don't we?"

"Yes, we do." They shared a bond, and always had, except he hadn't realized that until now. Something eased inside him.

"Sam?" she said, hesitation evident in her tone.

"Yes?"

"I...understand why you have to be careful with...a romantic relationship, and I respect that. Your kids are the priority and always will be, and that's as it should be. I just hope that your situation with Teresa won't affect my relationship with the twins. I really like spending time with them, and I don't want to lose that."

Her worry about her bond with Nicky and Rosie had a warm spot radiating from his chest outward. No surprise she would be concerned about the twins. That, it seemed, was the way she rolled. "I would never keep them from knowing you."

"Oh, good," she said, her shoulders sagging. "I'd be so sad if I couldn't see them ever again."

He tapped a finger on the steering wheel, thinking about what had been left unsaid. "So, maybe I'm being presumptuous, but I want us to be on the same page. You seeing Nicky and Rosie is all we can let happen, right?"

"Oh, right," she replied right away, nodding. "And, really, that's best all around. I have to focus on Happy Endings and you have to focus on what's best for the kids. That doesn't leave room for much else, does it?"

"No, it doesn't," he replied, determined not to sound disappointed. Reality couldn't be ignored, not with so much at stake. He then added, "I respect you too much not to speak the truth."

"I agree," she said with a touch of brusqueness. "And thank you for your respect. It goes both ways." She gathered up her purse and smoothed her coat.

"Good to know we understand each other."

"It is, isn't it?" she said with a bright edge to her voice. "Makes it easier all around."

"Exactly."

"Well, then, glad we got that figured out." She gave him a close-lipped smile that, to his thinking, didn't quite reach her pretty eyes, and then opened the door and got out. She turned and bent down to look at him through the open door. Her hair slid down to touch her smooth cheeks, and the wind picked up the strands and blew them around her face. "Well, thanks for the ride, Sam. I appreciate it."

"You're welcome," he said, wishing he could reach out and rub her silky-looking hair between his fingers. "Don't work too long."

"Only until the work's done."

"Of course. Happy Endings is your priority." For good reason. He couldn't fault her for that.

"Yes, it is, so I better get to it." She shut the door with a *clunk,* waved and turned and went to the store's doorway under the wide awning.

While she unlocked the door, he stayed put to be sure she got in safely. The door opened and she slipped inside without a look back and closed it behind her. He sat, still watching, and briefly saw her standing inside through the open blinds. And then, after a moment, the blinds rotated shut and she was gone from sight.

And Sam was alone in the dark with nothing but the hollow sound of the rain, the low howl of the wind and the lingering scent of peaches to keep him company.

Chapter Nine

Saturday dawned sunny, with just the vestiges of the rain from the night before left on the street. Allison arrived at Happy Endings a little after dawn to continue working on inventory data entry. She had to get the numbers entered so she could relax a tad—until the next challenge popped up.

Bring it on, she thought. Working made her feel worthwhile. Needed. Part of something meaningful, and with the town's well-being involved, she was an integral part of something bigger than simply what she wanted for herself. She couldn't ask for much more.

She dutifully kept thoughts of Sam in the back of her mind, where they belonged. He was a distraction she could not afford, especially after they'd talked last night. It would be easy to get caught up in the wounds they shared, but she wouldn't let that happen, especially now that she knew he wouldn't, either, what with Teresa's custody threats hanging over him. So as long as Allison could see the twins once in a while, she'd be content. An auntlike relationship with the two darlings would be enough. It had to be.

As opening approached—Viv had the morning off—Allison dusted all the shelves and cleaned the front windows to be sure everything looked sparkling clean and inviting.

Then she hurried to the Cozy Cup for a cup of Josh's wonderful coffee to fortify herself for the busy day to come. She thanked Josh profusely for his computer help, said hello to Chase Rollins, who owned Fluff & Stuff pet store just two doors down from her shop, and then, coffee cup in hand, hurried back toward Happy Endings. She waved to Mayor Langston across the street in front of city hall, and he saluted her with the cane he carried.

She arrived back at the store and quickly

dusted the front counter. She then opened the store precisely at the stroke of ten, pleased to see Miss Ann Mars was already waiting on the sidewalk for Allison to unlock the doors.

"Well, good morning, Miss Mars," Allison shouted so the older woman could hear her. Miss Mars, who was in her early eighties by now, had lived in Bygones for as long as Allison could remember, and was a member of the SOS Committee. She operated This 'N' That, a sundries/thrift/flea market–type establishment across Main Street from Happy Endings. She seemed quite content to live in an apartment over the store. Allison and Lori had loved going to Miss Mars's shop when they were growing up to hunt for trinkets and treasures. In fact, Allison still had an inexpensive but lovely beaded purse she'd bought there with the allowance money she'd saved all summer long when she was thirteen.

"Good morning, Miss True," Miss Mars chirped. She had her powder-white hair coiled up into a bundle on her small head and wore a flower-print dress that hung on her thin, stooped frame. But her eyes were as bright and inquisitive as ever.

"What can I help you with today?" Allison inquired.

Miss Mars waved a bony hand. "Oh, well, I saw the lights on here late last night and quite early this morning, so I wanted to come by to see how things were going. Part of my SOS Committee duties, you see."

"I appreciate your stopping by." Allison gestured around the store, glad she'd cleaned. "As you can see, everything is going well," she said, trying to put a positive spin on things. Business needed to pick up, though, if the store were to stay afloat. Which it would if she had anything to say about it.

As if to punctuate that thought, the bells over the door rang, heralding the arrival of a customer. Allison looked over and observed Helen Langston, Mayor Langston's wife and proprietor of the Hometown Grocery, enter the store, holding her head at its usual imperious angle. She was a tall, thin woman with an ever-thinner repertoire of social skills, though she ran a mean cash register at the grocery store, and had for years.

"Oh, you have a customer." Miss Mars shooed Allison away. "Go, dear." She pursed her thin lips. "But…could you just point me in the direction of the romance novels?"

"Why, Miss Mars, I didn't know you were an aficionado of the romance genre."

"Oh, well, I do like reading a good love story now and then." Her eyes sparkled. "Who doesn't love a *happy ending?*"

Allison raised her eyebrows, impressed by Miss Mars's play on words. "Ah, very clever, Miss Mars, alluding to my store. Good one." The old woman was sharper than she looked, and Allison hoped she had half Miss Mars's quick wit when she was pushing eighty-five. "The romances are in the back left corner. Would you like me to take you there?"

"Oh, no, my dear. I'll simply browse as I go, if you don't mind. I also love a good mystery now and again, so I'll look at those, too."

"Excellent," Allison said. "They're one aisle over from the romances."

With a wave, Miss Mars toddled away toward the back of the store.

Allison watched her go, then headed toward Mrs. Langston, thinking about what Miss Mars had said. Yes, everyone liked a happy ending in a romance novel, herself included, Allison mused. But she was determined to keep any romantic happy endings where they belonged—firmly entrenched between the covers of the books she sold.

On Saturday evening, Sam left the kids at home with Shawna so he could run a few errands solo. Dragging the kids shopping didn't make much sense, especially when time was short with most of the stores in town closing soon.

He parked at the Hometown Grocery, went in and picked up a few staples, noting as he did that Helen Langston was her usual stiff self and had her eye on the clock the whole time he was there. Yeah, close to quitting time. She had her brunette hair pulled back into a bun, which to Sam always looked so tight it was a wonder she could smile. Maybe that was why she never did.

As he shopped, feeling funny pushing the teeny-tiny cart around the store, he found himself wishing that the shop hadn't shut down its butchery department when the town had started its downward spiral. But with people pulling up stakes and other businesses shutting their doors, the Langstons' decision about closing down the butchery made sense. Unfortunately, Sam now had to go into the town of Manhattan for meat. Guess grilled cheese would have to do for a while. Fortunately, the twins loved that meal, along with boxed macaroni and cheese, which the Hometown Grocery fortunately carried.

With the time still in mind, he paid and left, then threw the groceries in the back of his SUV and walked hastily by city hall. He headed across the intersection of Main Street and Bronson Avenue on his way to the Fixer-Upper to pick up a few items he needed for around the house. At this hour on a Saturday, Main Street was quiet, save for a few kids at the far end skateboarding.

Once on Main Street he determinedly kept on going right past Happy Endings— he wasn't in need of reading material, now, was he?—and arrived at the Fixer-Upper right before closing.

Patrick Fogerty, a man about Sam's age, was the proprietor of the store, and, as such, a newcomer to Bygones. Sam had met him at one of the preseason basketball games recently and liked him fine. Patrick greeted him with a firm handshake and, after discussing the basketball team's prospects that year, eagerly helped Sam find the items he needed. Sam was impressed by the selection at the store and wished Patrick well before he left.

Then he headed back to his SUV, doggedly keeping himself from looking in the window of Happy Endings to get a glimpse of Allison, though he was certain she was in there because the lights were on.

He reached his vehicle, got in and put his parcel on the passenger seat, noticing a flash of red on the floor. He looked more closely and discovered Allison's scarf lying there, half under the passenger seat. She must have forgotten it when she'd left his SUV last night.

Unable to help himself, he raised the soft scarf to his nose and inhaled. The scent of freshly picked peaches hit him, and he stopped a noisy sigh just in time.

The scent brought to mind her ready smile, and without thinking much about what he was doing, he got back out of the SUV, scarf in hand, and retraced his steps to Main Street.

Soon he found himself standing outside Happy Endings. A closed sign hung in the front window, but he noted again that the lights were still on. Maybe Allison was missing her scarf? He knocked.

She opened the door. "Why, Sam. I didn't expect to see you here." She wore a well-fitting pair of black pants and a blue top that highlighted the lovely color of her eyes. Maybe it was a trick of the light, but he thought he saw some very faint dark circles shadowing the tops of her cheeks. She was obviously working some very long hours.

He held up the scarf. "You left this in my car."

"Ah, I was wondering where that went."

He handed it to her. "I thought you might be."

"Thanks," she said, taking the scarf. "How are the kids?"

"Good. They're home with a sitter so I can get some errands done."

"Oh, I see." She stepped back. "Actually, I got a new shipment of books recently and found a couple I'd like to send home with you for the twins." She gestured him in.

"You didn't have to do that," he said, following her lead. What a thoughtful woman.

She shut the door behind him. "I know, but I wanted to."

He paused, amazed at how quickly the kids had become included in her circle. "Well, they love to be spoiled."

As she headed over to the front counter, she turned and said, "And I love spoiling them." She put the scarf on the counter, went behind it and bent down, then came back up with a bag in her hands.

He moved closer as a thought occurred to

him. "Wouldn't you like to give these to them yourself?"

"I...um, would that be okay?"

"Of course." He furrowed his brow. "Why wouldn't it be?"

"I don't know." One hand came up and fiddled with a lock of hair near her chin. "I just don't want to...step on any toes."

He thought on that a moment, and then her reasoning became clear. And he didn't like what he'd deduced. "Ah, I see where this is going. You're worried about Teresa."

"A bit, maybe."

"While I appreciate your concern, I told you that you could see the kids anytime you wanted, and I meant it." *He* was the one who needed to stay uninvolved with Allison. Not Nicky and Rosie. "They adore you." And he couldn't blame them.

Allison chewed on her bottom lip. "I know—maybe I could give the books to them at church tomorrow."

He stiffened. "I don't take the kids to church."

"O-oh." A frown marred her brow. "I

didn't know. I haven't seen you at the Sunday service, so I just assumed you went to the Wednesday night service."

"Nope." He flattened his lips. "I haven't gone to church in a really long time."

"What? Why?" She shook her head. "You and Lori and your dad went to church all the time when we were growing up—I went to services with you since my parents didn't have time. In fact, I remember wanting to go to youth group just because I knew you'd be there."

He swallowed. "See, the thing is, ever since Teresa left, I don't have much faith in God anymore." He missed God, but didn't know how to reconnect.

"Oh, wow," Allison said, her brow crinkling. "What happened?"

Sam thought about that. "When my mom left, all of us hung on to our faith for dear life. But when Teresa abandoned me and the kids, all I could think about was that a truly merciful God wouldn't let the same thing happen to me again."

"So…it sounds like you're angry with God?"

He considered that. "Yes, I guess I am." In fact, just after Teresa left, he'd been downright furious with Him.

"I get that," she said, her voice soft and edged with empathy.

"You do?" he asked, surprised she understood.

"Oh, yeah." She leaned a hip against the counter. "About the time I graduated from high school and my parents were nowhere to be found, I went through a period when I felt sorry for myself, and I was mad at God, too, for not answering my prayers about my home situation." She drew in a shaky breath. "But then I realized my anger was creating distance between me and God, and that because of that distance, I felt more alone than ever."

"I'm so sorry you had to go through that." She understood, though, more than he'd realized, and that warmed some places inside him that had felt numb for months.

"Thanks," she said. "But I'm in a better

place now that I've let myself rely on God. I don't feel as…alone."

"I get the alone thing. I've felt that way since Teresa left." Of course, he was surrounded by people every day at work, and he had the twins at home some of the time. But emotionally, he'd been on his own for a long time. "Sometimes I wonder if my faith has deserted me."

"Your faith is still there, Sam. It never went anywhere."

His breathing stalled.

She went on. "I've learned by my experiences that faith, by its very nature, never leaves someone who truly believes in the Lord."

He digested what she'd said. "I…I do believe in God." That had never changed, never wavered.

"Then look inside for your faith and you'll be fine."

"What you've said makes a lot of sense." He smiled, feeling a weight lift from his heart. "Thank you for helping me figure some of this out."

"Glad I could help. But it might help more if you came to church tomorrow." She pressed her lips into an impish grin. "It is God's house, after all. What better place to reconnect with Him?"

"You might be right." Sam nodded as the idea grew on him just a bit.

"And I'm sure the kids would love Sunday school. It would be a bonus for those two darling munchkins."

His heart turned over at her mention of the twins, but, then, her concern for them always touched him. "You know, you're right."

"And I'd enjoy seeing them to give them their books." She held up the bag. "I'll take them with me, and if you guys are there, I'll be sure and come over and say hi."

"I'll have to think on it." And he would. Long and hard. Probably well into the night.

For in the back of his mind he realized that going to church would not only hopefully help him build a stronger bond with God, but it would also allow him to see Allison again. And thoughts like those treaded dangerously close to swirling waters he had to avoid.

* * *

The next morning, Allison arrived at church a bit early, the bag holding the twins' books in hand.

Lily Bronson, a tall willowy blonde around Allison's age, hailed her down in the church's small vestibule. "Allison. I haven't seen you in a while. I've been meaning to come by and get another look at what you've done with your store." Lily, a lawyer by training turned fabulous florist, had moved to Bygones from Boston in July, the last of the SOS shop owners to arrive in town.

Allison had liked Lily from the moment she met her, and since they were around the same age, planned on getting to know her better when she had more time to focus on something other than getting Happy Endings up and running. "Please do stop by. I've ordered a few books on flower design you might be interested in."

Lily pushed her tortoiseshell glasses back onto their perch on her nose. "How nice of you! I'll make it a priority to stop by soon. Actually, I also wanted to ask you what kind of flowers you'd like in your bouquet this week."

Since Lily had opened Love in Bloom, she'd impressed the whole town with her unique flower arrangements, including an inspired concoction she'd made for Happy Endings for the grand opening of all the businesses. The bouquet had been comprised of flowers spilling out of an old typewriter Lily had unearthed at the This 'N' That. Allison had decided to put in a weekly order to refresh the bouquet, and she liked to switch up the flowers she used.

"Well, I was thinking since the harvest festival is just around the corner, I'd like to have a fall theme in the bouquet this week."

Lily smiled. "Oh, what an excellent idea. I've ordered some lovely mums that would look beautiful in that kind of arrangement."

"Whatever you want to do, I know it will be spectacular."

Tate Bronson, Lily's brand-new husband—they'd been married at the beginning of the month after a short engagement—arrived on the scene, dressed in his Sunday best. "She does have a way with flowers, doesn't she?" he asked, his eyes lingering on Lily's face as he put his arm around her narrow shoulders.

Tate, who'd been widowed when his wife died while giving birth to their daughter, Isabella, was a descendant of the Bronson brothers who'd founded Bygones back in 1870. He was tall and strong looking, and had short, thick, dark brown hair and clear coffee-colored eyes. And he was obviously madly in love with his new wife, whom he'd met while serving as her SOS Committee liaison when she'd arrived in Bygones in July. Love had followed, and now they were the happiest set of newlyweds around, and Lily, Allison knew, was thrilled to be Isabella's new mom.

Another happy ending, Allison thought with a familiar pang.

"I also want to stop by and look at some books for Isabella. I've told her about Nancy Drew, and she's interested in reading those," Lily said.

"Oh, I love Nancy Drew." Allison grinned. "I devoured those books when I was a girl. I have several copies of *The Secret of the Old Clock* in stock, so I'll set one aside for her."

"Thank you so much," Lily said. "They might be a little above her reading level, but I thought it would be fun to read the books together, just to give her a taste."

"Excellent idea," Allison replied. "Seems like you've taken to motherhood like a pro."

Tate piped in, "She's a wonderful mother." He rubbed the top of Lily's arm. "I couldn't have asked for a better mom for Isabella."

She talked to Lily and Tate for a few more minutes and finished up the conversation awed and a little envious of the love they'd found. Maybe someday she could hope to find something like they had. Down the road, perhaps, after she'd succeeded at the challenge of making Happy Endings a resounding success. But until then, she had to keep her attention on her business.

She looked at her watch, noting that the service was about to start. She went into the half-full sanctuary and sat in one of the wooden pews, her eyes on the rough wooden cross in back of the pulpit, which stood to one side. She did her best to focus on getting in a worshipping frame of mind, but once she was seated, her thoughts kept returning to Sam and the discussion they'd had last night when he'd brought her scarf back to her.

She'd been undeniably happy to see him, and had been so relieved when he'd confirmed that she was free to see the twins. But it was their conversation about God that had really made an impression on her. Hearing about Sam's struggles in that area had just about broken her heart. He obviously felt alone without the Lord in his life, and that made her sad.

She hoped he'd come to church, but she was determined not to expect him to show up or be too disappointed if he didn't. He had to do things on his own timeline, in his own way, and she wasn't going to push. But she could pray for Sam, so she folded her hands in her lap and closed her eyes.

Lord, help Sam to find his way back to You, and help me to stay focused on the challenge I've been given with the bookstore.

Someone slid in next to her.

She turned to say hello. And words stuck in her mouth.

Sam.

"What, you didn't expect me to come?" he asked with a lift of one dark eyebrow.

Happiness rocketed through her and she resisted the urge to grab his hand and hold on to him for the whole service. Not a good idea. "Um...I was hoping you might, but...I wasn't sure."

He always looked handsome, but she'd never seen him in a suit and tie, and...wow, just wow. The dark blue color of the well-cut garment, paired with the white dress shirt he wore with a light blue regimental striped tie, brought out the golden glints in his eyes perfectly and set off the strong bone structure of his face in just the right way.

He settled next to her, unbuttoning his jacket.

She smelled his aftershave, all warm and spicy. Manly. Devastating, if she let it be. She wouldn't.

"Well, I thought a lot about what you said, and I decided you were right," he said. "I need to let my anger go and find a way to have God in my life again, the sooner the better."

Feeling warm, she took off her coat. "I'm glad," she said, then cast her gaze around. "The twins?"

"I already took them to the Sunday school classroom."

"How were they with it?" Sometimes new environments were difficult for kids to deal with.

"Fine." He reached for the bible in the shelf in front of them. "Rosie found the dolls and Nicky scoped out the toy trucks and that was that."

The organ rang out the beginning chords of a hymn, signaling the start of the service.

"Good," Allison whispered. "They'll have fun." And she'd get to worship with an old friend by her side. How could that be bad?

Pastor Garman stepped up to the pulpit and began the service by having everyone stand for the first hymn. The organ swelled around the congregation and Sam rose and held out his hymnal for Allison to share. His baritone voice rang out, and a memory surfaced in Allison—he had a terrible voice, no sense of tune at all. Completely tone-deaf.

She looked at him, blinking, and he just shrugged as if to say, "Hey, I never promised I could sing."

With a small smile, she inclined her head slightly in acknowledgment. No, he hadn't promised perfect singing. And something about a tone-deaf guy who sang anyway was seriously adorable. If she were noticing.

Despite Sam's out-of-tune singing during the song—and she used the word *singing* broadly—a wonderful sense of calm came over Allison. Being in church, a place of worship, singing her praises to God, had always soothed her and given her the sense of belonging and acceptance she hadn't ever had at her parents' home.

And having Sam here, sharing in her praise, made the service doubly special.

When the hymn was over, the congregation sat, and Pastor Garman delivered the sermon on forgiveness from the lectern in the pulpit. Allison listened intently, as she always did, trying to take a nugget from the sermon to contemplate later.

After the sermon, Pastor Garman bade the congregation to stand, and the strains of the beginning chords of "Love Lifted Me," one of Allison's favorite hymns, rose in the church. Sam opened the hymnal to the correct page.

She stole a look at Sam as the song went on, noting he wasn't looking at the hymnal. He was clearly familiar with the song.

The organ played the last chord and the service ended. The members of the congregation started exiting the pews.

Sam turned to Allison.

She spoke before he did. "You knew the words to that hymn."

"Yeah, I remembered them from when I was younger."

She gestured for him to head to the center aisle of the church. "Do you believe them?"

"What? The words?"

"Yes."

He stopped when he reached the center aisle, his head cocked sideways. "I...don't know."

"'He will lift you by His love, out of the angry waves,'" she sang.

Sam hesitated, clearly digesting the lyrics. "Ah. I see. Kind of like a personal message to me?"

Allison moved by his side up the aisle toward the back of the church, melding with the other parishioners. "Timely, I'd say, huh? God knows what one needs to hear, and when."

Sam paused, then said, "I like that thought."

"I'm so glad." Allison saw Viv waving her over to the left side of the church. "Oh, Viv wants to talk to me. I'll meet you in the vestibule so I can give the kids their books."

"Okay, see you there," Sam replied, turning to head toward the back of the church.

Allison watched him go, undeniably happy he'd come today.

He was still in the early stages of rediscovering his faith and his connection with God. She hoped he found his way. For himself, and, of course, for the twins, too. Though she and Sam could never be more than friends, she wanted what was best for the Franklin family and always would.

Chapter Ten

Sam left Allison's side and said hello to Scott and his parents, Karen and Wes Martin. He waved to Julia Fleming, who taught social studies at Bygones High, and had a word with Dale Eversleigh, the town undertaker, about how the basketball team was coming along. As they discussed the schedule, it hit home to Sam how much he liked that the whole town supported the team. He just couldn't imagine leaving to teach and coach somewhere else. He desperately hoped that would never come to pass.

Thoughts of Bygones had him looking around the vestibule at the clusters of parishioners talking. The sense of community en-

veloped him like an old friend, and suddenly
he was so glad he'd gone with the decision
he'd made at 3:00 a.m. last night to attend the
church service this morning.

There was comfort here in God's house.
Peace and solace. All things he needed. Desperately. Which had been hit home by Allison's statement.

*He knows what one needs to hear, and
when.*

As he went to get a glass of water from the
carafe set out on a table in the corner, com-
prehension shot through him like an inbound
pass. Her words were so true. Part of Sam
had forgotten about the sense of serenity and
rightness that always took hold of him when
he worshipped here, when he talked to God
and God listened.

A moment later, Allison and Viv appeared
in the vestibule. He watched them over the
rim of his water glass, his heart kick-starting
at just the sight of Allison. She looked very
pretty today, dressed in dark slacks and a
knee-length emerald-green coat that really set

off her dark hair. She had such a fresh beauty about her, so uncontrived and natural, so—

"Well, I haven't seen you here in quite a while."

He turned. "You're right about that, Coraline." She looked as smart as she always did, dressed in her Sunday finery, which included a black wool coat over a bright red sweater and a black, knee-length skirt. Her short gray hair was styled perfectly, as always.

She looked away from him, her razor-sharp blue gaze zeroing in on Allison. "Dare I say that Miss True had something to do with your return to the fold?"

Coraline's perceptiveness always threw him a little. She always seemed to...*know* things. But...she was a matchmaker, and it was obvious where this was going—straight to the altar, if Coraline had anything to say about it.

"Um...well." He cleared his throat as he scrunched his eyebrows together. "Why do you say that?" Maybe if he played dumb she'd back off. She meant well, but he had to stay strong.

Coraline gave him a beatific smile. "Anyone with eyes would be able to see that you're taken with her. The rest was just a matter of making a connection."

Taken with Allison? Oh, wow. Not what he wanted. He needed to be more careful. "Oh, we're just friends."

Coraline's blue eyes twinkled. "Really?"

"Yes," he insisted. "She's been helping me out with the twins."

"So they like her?"

"Oh, yes. They love her."

"She's a wonderful woman," Coraline said. "I hear you have some of your athletes involved in Allison's writing workshops."

"Yes, Rory Liston and Scott Martin."

"Excellent." Coraline nodded.

"Allison will be a good influence on your children."

"I agree." Wholeheartedly.

Coraline studied him. "I feel that God has another plan for you. Something wonderful."

Something wonderful. Unexpected yearning spread through him but he batted it back.

"I'm not quite sure what to say to that," he replied in all honesty.

"I'll pray about it, if you don't mind."

"Of course not." Prayers couldn't hurt. But reality was much more difficult to ignore.

"Good. And I hope you'll continue to come to church."

"I will. I feel closer to God here, and I'm glad I came because I need Him right now."

"Excellent." With a warm smile, Coraline went off toward the front doors of the church, which had been flung open wide to let in the October sun. She greeted Robert Randall, the owner of the now-defunct Randall Manufacturing.

Sam stood alone for a few moments, wondering about what Coraline had said.

I feel that God has another plan for you. Something wonderful.

Was it possible her words were true? And was he a complete fool, or even worse yet, a bad father, for even considering the validity of Coraline's statement?

If so, he had a lot of thinking to do. And Allison was at the center of it all.

Chapter Eleven

"The end."

Allison closed the book she'd read for the kids, her eyes on the woman who'd come to Story Time a bit late, four kids in tow, including Nicky and Rosie.

Lori! Lori was here. With her own kids, and her niece and nephew.

Smiling, Allison rose and hustled over to where Lori stood. "It is so good to see you, Lor," she said, automatically reverting to her nickname for her best childhood friend. Save for shorter, slightly darker hair, Lori looked the same as Allison remembered, all freckles and caramel-colored, long-lashed eyes Allison had always envied.

Lori grinned back and opened her arms. "You, too, old friend."

They embraced, and Allison felt as if a missing piece of her heart had been replaced. She and Lori had shared everything at one time, their hopes and dreams most of all. Allison realized at this moment how much she'd missed Lori, how big a hole the loss of her friendship had caused. She'd wanted to reconnect, but something had always held her back.

When they pulled apart, Allison saw tears in Lori's eyes. In reaction, her own eyes burned. "Hey, now." She blinked a few times. "Don't make me cry at work."

Lori laughed. "Sorry. It's just so great to see you."

"And you, too." She gestured to the Kids' Korner, where the four children looked at books Allison had set on the table, two towheads and two brunettes. "I take it those are your kids over there with Nicky and Rosie."

Motherly pride and unconditional love glowed in Lori's eyes. "Yes. Those are my babies. Katy is three going on ten and Jacob is four."

"Wow." Allison gazed at the two blond cherubs with their round rosy cheeks. "They're gorgeous."

"Thanks. They're a handful, but I love them to pieces."

"You're very happy, right?" Allison said.

"Yes, I am."

A cold spot in Allison's chest throbbed, taking her off guard. She just nodded.

"Listen, I'm watching Nicky and Rosie this afternoon—Sam's ex flaked out again—and I was going to take the kids to the Cozy Cup Café for some hot cocoa. You want to go with us so you and I can catch up?"

"What a wonderful idea, especially considering I finally have a pesky inventory-control problem resolved." Allison had had some late nights and early mornings spent trying to figure that mess out. Thankfully she'd waded through the problem and had come out the other side with a system that worked, along with a huge sense of accomplishment. "It wouldn't hurt for me to take a small break. Let me go make sure Viv, my employee, will be okay on her own for a bit."

"Your employee." Lori shook her head as she looked around. "I can't believe you own this place."

"I'm very blessed," Allison said. "This is what I've always wanted." Nothing had changed there.

She let Viv know she'd be gone for a bit, and then she and Lori herded the kids to the Cozy Cup Café. The day was cloudy but dry, and it felt good to get some fresh air after being cooped up in the store since early this morning.

This late in the afternoon the small café, which lived up to its name by being very cozy and inviting, was empty, so Allison and Lori had their pick of tables.

Once they got the kids settled at a spot by the window, Lori left Allison with the youngsters while she went up and got coffee for her, tea for Allison and hot cocoa for the kids. She engaged the kids in a lively discussion about the stories she'd read at Story Time, and then Lori was back, bearing hot drinks for all, along with delicious-looking pastries. Lori gave each of the kids a pastry and cocoa, then sat next to Allison. "I'm starved," she said, taking a pastry.

"Me, too," Allison replied, digging into her own doughnut.

They made small talk for a few minutes while they ate, and then Lori eyed Allison, one eyebrow cocked. "So I've heard that you and Sam have reconnected."

Allison almost choked on her coffee. "Um… yeah." She cleared her throat. "He and the kids have been coming to Story Time," she said truthfully. They hadn't spent any time alone. No risk there.

"So it's all about the kids?"

"Of course," Allison said evenly. "As it should be." Especially with Teresa's threats looming.

Lori regarded Allison for a long moment. "So did Sam tell you that he liked you way back in high school and wanted to ask you out?"

Allison's tummy flipped and she almost

dropped her pastry. "Nooo, he didn't tell me that."

"Yup, it's true."

"But he didn't ask me out," Allison said.

"I discouraged him."

This was news. "What?" Allison furrowed her brow. "Why?"

"He was leaving for college in the fall and I was worried you'd get hurt."

"So you were watching out for me?"

"Uh-huh. Plus, I admit I was worried our friendship would be affected if you went out with him and it didn't work out."

"Oh, wow."

"Are you mad?" Lori asked.

Allison thought about that. It would make sense for her to be mad at Lori for what she'd done, but that had all happened a long time ago, and she wasn't the type to hold a grudge. What good would that do? "No, not now. I've moved on."

"Oh, good. I've always felt guilty about my part in discouraging him."

Pieces of the puzzle came together for Allison. "Is your guilt the reason you haven't contacted me since I've been back?"

"Partly, yes," Lori said sheepishly. "Plus, we were in Oregon for two months, visiting Joe's family there, and we just got back last week."

"I think Sam mentioned that."

"Can you forgive me for meddling, and for not contacting you?"

"Of course. The phone works both ways, so I guess we're even." Allison stirred her tea. "And, I have to admit, I've been working on getting the store up and running and haven't had time for any kind of social life."

"The bookstore is important to you, isn't it?" Lori asked after she took a bite of pastry.

"It's everything." Nutshell explanation, but dead-on.

"Yeah, a lot's riding on the SOS Committee's plan working. Bygones needs Main Street to be successful."

"Yes, there's that, but…I also want to make Happy Endings work for a lot of other reasons."

"Such as?" Lori asked.

"Such as, my parents told me I'd fail when I left town, and for ten years I did, flitting from job to job until I started at the Book Barn, never feeling fulfilled, never finding the right fit, never sticking it out. Now I have the opportunity to succeed and prove them wrong. I need that, I need to know I can make this work, that I have what it takes."

"With that attitude, I have every confidence you'll make that bookstore just what Bygones, and you, need."

"You always did understand me."

"And you understood me," Lori said. "I've missed that."

"Me, too."

A squabble broke out between Jacob and Katy, and Lori diverted her attention to referee. To Allison's amazement, Nicky and Rosie both sat quietly, eating. Food. The great distraction.

Once she had her kids calmed down, Lori turned back to Allison. "Can I let you in on a little secret?"

Allison leaned forward. "Of course, I love a good secret. Spill."

"I was kind of hoping that now maybe you and Sam might get together as more than friends."

Another shocker. "You were?" Allison asked, managing to keep her voice neutral, even as Lori's statement sent yearning ricocheting around inside her.

"Yep. You guys would make a great couple."

A couple. Her and Sam. Just the thought of that had Allison's heart tripping over itself. She paid no attention. Well, hardly any. "That's never going to happen." Allison wanted to ask Lori if she knew about Teresa's threat, but she didn't; that wasn't Allison's story to tell.

"Why not?" Lori asked, her gaze intent.

"Well, I can't speak for Sam, but I'm not looking for romance. And, um, I don't think Sam is, either."

Lori nodded as she chewed on her bottom lip. "Well, I guess you're right about that. Sam isn't exactly gung-ho on love after what happened with Teresa."

"Believe me, he and I are on the same page right now."

"Maybe, but I know Sam is lonely. Who wouldn't be, what with a demanding job and twins to take care of at home, even part-time? I've always wanted him to find another woman to share his life with."

A pang of hope knotted Allison's stomach, but she did her best to minimize the emotion. Allowing herself to hope for anything with Sam was futile. And foolish, for a lot of good reasons. She knew this and couldn't forget it. "He told me he doesn't believe in romantic love."

"He did?" Lori asked, sitting up straighter, her eyes wide. "You guys have actually talked about this?"

"Don't get your hopes up," Allison said, waving a hand in the air. She'd be sure to take her own advice. "The subject came up in a conversation we were having about your dad having never remarried."

"Oh." Lori slumped. "Rats."

Allison waved to Patrick Fogerty, owner of the Fixer-Upper, who stood at the front counter with his new fiancée, Gracie Wilson, ordering from Josh. Then Allison returned her attention to Lori. "He told me it was because of Teresa."

Lori nodded. "And my mom," Lori said flatly. "Sam hasn't ever really forgotten her abandonment. And neither have I."

Allison touched Lori's hand. "I know." She and Lori had talked about Doris Franklin's desertion many times when they were growing up, and Allison had held Lori more than once as she'd sobbed after her mom had left one hot summer day when they were nine. "We both had crummy mothers." Lori was the one person who had an idea about Allison's neglectful parents.

"True." Lori paused as she mopped up some milk Katy had spilled. "Still, maybe he'll come around—"

"No, he won't, and neither will I," Allison said with velvet-coated steel in her voice. "He has his reasons, and so do I. There's no chance we'll ever get together. You have to quit hoping for that, Lor. It's the only sensible thing to do."

Lori opened her mouth to respond.

But Nicky squawked and said, "Don't boss me, Ro-ro," and Rosie gave an indignant squeal of her own, and then tried to steal some of Nicky's doughnut, signaling to Allison that her and Lori's window of calm had closed. The troops were restless and the grown-ups' discussion was at an end.

With a significant look, Lori stood and went over to break up the skirmish between her niece and nephew. Allison sat for a moment, pondering. Allison had talked the talk about her and Sam. Now she needed to walk the walk and put Sam where he belonged.

Out of hope's range. For good.

Allison stood in the aisle of the Hometown Grocery, pondering what kind of laundry detergent to buy. Not that she had a ton of choices here, but there were a few, at least. And given that she was on a budget, she liked to be sure she chose the best value.

Deciding on the bargain brand, she set the bottle in the cart and then turned to head to the dairy aisle. Only to come face-to-face with her mom.

"Mom," she squeaked.

"Allison," her mother said with a stiff nod. She had her gray-streaked dark hair scraped back into its usual tight bun, wore zero makeup and was dressed in jeans and a baggy T-shirt that Allison knew for a fact were from the late eighties. To say that Vera True was a minimalist was an understatement. In everything she did, including raising her kids.

"I'm surprised to see you here." Her mom usually did her shopping on a weekend once a month at a large warehouse store in nearby Manhattan, and had stuck to that schedule down to the hour for as long as Allison could remember. Plus, Dad kept a strict budget that didn't allow for a lot of convenience shopping at the smaller, more expensive Hometown Grocery.

"Well, I was sick with a cold last weekend and couldn't make my usual trip to Manhattan, so I just decided to swing in and pick up a few things here."

"Are you feeling better now?" Allison dutifully asked. Not much brought her mom down physically, so she must have really been feeling lousy if she'd strayed from her usual routine.

"Yes, I'm fine. Just a little stuffed up."

"Oh. Good." Allison hesitated, searching for common ground. "Um…Amy is coming to the writing workshops I've been holding at the store."

Mom sniffed. If Allison didn't know better, she would have thought the sniff was because of the cold. "Yes, I know. She hasn't been around to do her chores."

Ah. Of course. Each of the girls had an extensive chore list every week, and Mom was notoriously inflexible with deviations. "Well, it will help her grades, so maybe the chores will keep," Allison said carefully.

"Perhaps," Mom said, which was the code word she used when she disagreed but didn't want to have a confrontation. Very passive-aggressive, as far as Allison was concerned, given her mom was well aware that Allison knew the code. "So how are things going with your little store?"

Allison gritted her teeth at the words *little store*. She'd heard that expression before, the last time she'd talked to her parents, just after she'd moved back and had driven out to the farm to say hi to her sisters. "Pretty well, actually," she said with a lift of her chin. "I haven't failed yet, as you thought I would."

"Well, come and let me know how things are going in three years or so." Mom pressed her lips into a thin line. "Running a business in the long term is nonstop work, and a lot harder than most people think."

"I'm well aware, Mom. I watched you and Dad all those years, remember?"

"Yes, I guess you are aware." Mom paused. "Maybe that's why we're so unsupportive."

"What do you mean?"

"Well, we know what it's like trying to make a business successful, how grueling it is. Maybe we wanted something different for you."

Allison blinked. "Is that true? Because that's not what you said when I told you I was moving back. You said, and I quote, 'Well, don't come running to us when you fail.'"

Mom blanched, her mouth working. But then she steadied her jaw and set it at a slight yet unmistakable angle. "Perhaps it's true."

Allison shook her head and rolled her eyes. Oh, how she hated that word *perhaps*. But that was the way her parents did things— throw an idea out and then snatch it back with something noncommittal. Something that wouldn't require any kind of emotional pledge.

Well, she wasn't going to change them now, and she wasn't up for some roundabout conversation that would end the way it always did when her parents were involved—with them expressing their reservations rather than their support. She was through going in circles with them. "Okay, I get the picture. You've made your opinion clear." Or not. Either way, Allison vowed to break free of letting their viewpoint matter.

"We just don't want to see you go through the agony of watching what you've worked so hard for falter."

"Did it ever occur to you that I might not fail?" Allison snorted. "After all, I've got the workaholic example to follow in you and Dad."

Mom drew herself up. "We only did what was necessary to make the farm stay afloat," she said, her voice rife with defensiveness.

"And what about your kids, Mom? What did you do to help us stay afloat?"

Her mouth pruned up. "We gave you everything you needed."

"Except your love."

"Love is taking care of others, keeping a roof over their heads and food in their bellies."

This didn't surprise Allison; both her mom and dad had been raised by farmers who were long on physical work and short on emotional connection. They modeled that lifestyle with seeming ease, never deviating, never faltering. Never seeing the other side. "No, love is more than that. Love is taking care of emotional needs as well as physical ones."

Mom paused, her brow furrowed. "I don't know how to do that."

Something died a little more inside Allison. "I know you don't."

"You turned out pretty good," her mother whispered.

It was as close to a compliment as Allison would ever get. "Thanks."

Mom looked at her watch. "Oh, look at the time. I still have work to do at the office."

Lack of time was a recurrent theme with her mom. "And I have work to do at *my little store,*" Allison added.

Mom inclined her head in what looked like grudging admiration. More code? "Well, then, we both best get going."

"Yes, I suppose so," Allison replied. "Say hello to Dad for me, and Amanda and Amy, too."

"I will," Mom said, turning.

"Maybe you should stop by the store," Allison suggested. "I've done a lot with the space."

"Maybe we will, if we can fit it in." With those words she gave Allison a small smile and walked away, her back ramrod straight.

Something shriveled inside Allison. Time

to fit a visit in? It wasn't likely to happen. And she had to accept that and move on or she'd never be free from her parents.

But…was what her mom had said true? Had they warned her off from running her own business because they wanted a different life for her? Or had they been so harsh because they doubted her abilities? Was it possible she'd misjudged her parents all along?

She hated that she wondered even one tiny little bit.

Chapter Twelve

With a twin holding on to each of his hands, Sam headed from his SUV into the church, dodging raindrops. The day of the annual harvest festival had dawned rainy, but the wet weather hadn't dampened the twins' excitement about attending the festival. In fact, they'd talked about nothing else for the past few days. Sam couldn't figure out if they were more excited about the actual festival or the prospect of seeing Allison. In his mind, Allison won by a nose. They adored her.

The kids had begged to go to Story Time this week, and he hadn't been able to say no. And if there was anything that highlighted Allison's wonderful personality, it was seeing her in action with the kids. Every kind smile, every patient glance, every understanding touch she gave the kids made him notice her even more.

So, here they were at the harvest festival, with its plethora of fun booths, ranging from Allison's creative-writing workshop's literacy booth to food booths to craft booths brimming with handmade stuff that boggled his uncrafty mind, as well as a booth sponsored by each of the SOS Main Street businesses.

The basement of the church had been set up as it usually was for the annual festival, with booths ringing the perimeter of the low-ceilinged space. In the center, beneath some exposed pipes, was a bobbing-for-apples station, as well as a popcorn-stringing station and a pumpkin-carving station. The place smelled of cinnamon, apples and hay from the bales that had been set up in random spots for those who needed to sit.

The whole town showed up for the festival, which this year was serving as a fundraiser for the SOS Committee's endeavors. People milled around, talking and having fun and taking part in some good old-fashioned small-town socializing.

He saw Melissa Sweeney and her fiancé, Brian Montclair, manning a cupcake-decorating table, and Josh Smith had set up a small booth in one corner from which he was serving small cups of fragrant coffee. Sam would be sure and stop by all the booths before they left.

"Daddy, where is Miss Allison's booth?" Rosie asked.

Nicky tugged on Sam's hand. "Yeah, Daddy. We wanna go to her booth first."

Clearly, Miss Allison was the main event. He scoped the place out—one of the advantages of being taller than just about everybody else—and spied the literacy booth in the far left corner, sporting the colorful banner Viv had made. "Her booth is over there." He pointed left. "Let's go and say hi."

They wended their way through the throng, stopping briefly at the Everything booth to buy some of the hamburger sliders they were selling.

"How's the team shaping up?" Elwood Dill

asked, handing each of the kids and Sam a small burger served in a paper holder. He sported a long, graying beard, and under a bright yellow apron he wore a tie-dyed T-shirt.

"Fine, fine, thanks for asking," Sam said around bites of burger. He never tired of discussing the team he loved to coach. He doubted any other town would be so support-ive of his boys. "Rory Liston is shaping up to be a great center."

"He's a tall kid but needs some weight," Elwood said.

"I agree. He's been working in the weight room, so that should help." Sam patted his stomach. "I've been joining him when I can."

Elwood grunted. "Yeah, like you need it."

Velma swung her long gray hair over her shoulder as she chimed in, "We hope we don't lose you, Coach."

"Me, too, Velma." He gestured around. "But if this turnout is any indication, the SOS Committee's effort won't be in vain."

The kids finished their sliders and started fidgeting, so he bade goodbye to the Dills and headed over to the literacy booth, which Allison had combined with the Happy Endings booth.

Rory and Scott and a few other teens from the creative-writing class were expertly manning the booth.

"Yo, Coach," Rory said with a broad wave.

Sam gave him a thumbs-up and an approving nod.

Then Sam saw Allison standing guard in the background. She wore a snug pair of black jeans and a blue-green sweater that he could see even at a distance matched her eyes. She had her hair pulled back in a loose ponytail, and a few tendrils of hair had escaped to frame her face becomingly.

She spotted Sam and her face stilled, and then she smiled a welcoming smile—a slow rise of both sides of her mouth—that knocked him out at the knees. But he covered up his reaction by brandishing a casual wave. Hopefully he looked normal, not...smitten.

Oh, man. That's what he was. *Smitten.* Not good.

Before he could think about that idea for

much more than a second, the twins spotted her and ran over to greet her. Sam followed and watched as Allison hunkered down and hugged them in turn, lavishing attention on each of them, expertly treating them as individuals rather than as a twin unit as some people did.

She rose from hugging Nicky and looked at Sam. "Hey, you. Glad you could make it."

"Nothing would make me miss seeing Rory and Scott touting literacy in a skit," he said. "Usually it's all about basketball."

"Well, today it's all about reading and writing, and they're doing a fantastic job. The first performance went great," she said, nodding in the boys' direction. "You should be really proud."

"I am," he said. "You've done an amazing job with them." That was her way, being fantastic. Was there anything she couldn't accomplish?

Her cheeks colored. "It's been my pleasure."

Rosie piped in, "Daddy, I see *amnimals!*"

"Where?" Nicky said, going up on tiptoe, his head craned.

"Over there." Rosie pointed and danced in place. "Can we go see them?"

"That's the Fluff & Stuff booth," Allison said. "It's a popular one."

"Let's go take a look," Sam replied.

Nicky took Allison's hand. "You go with us, Miss Allison."

Rosie grabbed Allison's other hand. "Yeah. You can hold an *amnimal* with me."

Allison gave Sam a hesitant look. "Do you mind?"

He couldn't say that he did. "Not at all," he said. "Lead the way."

She headed toward the Fluff & Stuff booth, holding Rosie's and Nicky's hands, and Sam followed, admiring how she looked tending to his kids, as if she'd been born to nurture them.

He thought back to what he'd figured out. He was smitten with Allison. No question. Who wouldn't be? She was an extraordinary person in every way, and she showered his kids with love and attention that always had them glowing. In his book, that would always be a good thing. He'd hold on to that thought no matter what.

He was determined to make today all about the kids. If he kept that in mind, he couldn't go wrong.

On his way to the Fluff & Stuff booth, he spotted Whitney Leigh, who was furiously writing in a small notebook as she took in what was going on around her; she was clearly there in her official capacity as a reporter for the *Bygones Gazette*. He'd met her when she'd come to the school to interview him about the new math curriculum he'd implemented in September, so he felt obligated to say hello. "Good afternoon, Ms. Leigh."

She nodded brusquely. "Hello, Sam," she said in her no-nonsense way. She was a real go-getter and seemed set on making a journalistic name for herself in Bygones. She looked the part of serious reporter with her glasses and her blond hair pulled back in a neat-as-a-pin bun.

"Have you made any progress figuring out who the anonymous benefactor is?" Sam asked. It was common knowledge around town that she was intent on solving that mystery.

"Not yet." She shoved the pencil into her bun. "But I'm determined to get the real story."

"I guess the reporter side of you really needs to know."

"Yes, of course," she replied, nodding. "I've always felt the benefactor might have ulterior motives."

"Yes, I know." Back in July, Sam had heard the *Gazette*'s position that the benefactor, through the matching-grant mechanism, now owned half of downtown. According to her, that was real cause for concern for Bygones. Many townsfolk agreed with her.

She narrowed her eyes. "Do *you* know who it is?"

He held up his hands. "No sirree."

"Well," she said, jerking down the tailored black jacket she wore, "if you find out, be sure and let me know. I want that scoop."

He said he would, and then she yanked

the pencil out of her bun and left him with a terse, "Thank you."

When he arrived at the Fluff & Stuff booth, Allison knelt between Nicky and Rosie as they each held out their hands for Chase Rollins to hand them guinea pigs. Chase, who had a full head of black hair, was about thirty, Sam figured. He wasn't married and didn't have kids of his own, but he was a nice enough guy, if a bit quiet, in Sam's opinion.

Just as Chase was about to put the furry creature in Rosie's hands, she snatched them back. "I'm scared, Miss Allison." She turned and buried her head on Allison's shoulder.

Allison put her arms around Rosie, held her close and whispered in her ear.

Rosie nodded without looking up.

Allison looked at Chase. "Rosie would like me to hold the guinea pig, and she'll pet it that way, if that's okay."

"Sure thing, this little-girl guinea pig loves females," Chase said. "Here you go, Ms. True." He put the animal in Allison's out-stretched hands.

"See?" Allison said to Rosie. "She's very sweet and gentle."

Rosie peeked up at the animal in Allison's hands, and then tentatively reached out to touch the black-and-white guinea pig's fur. Her little bow-shaped mouth curved into a smile. "He's so soft!" she exclaimed.

"It's a she," Allison said. "Remember?"

"Oh, yeah." Rosie giggled. "I forgot."

Chase went over and got another guinea pig out of its cage, and then brought it back for Nicky, who had no compunction of any kind about holding the animal. But, then, he'd always been more adventurous than Rosie. His face lit up into a big smile when Chase gently set the black-and-white guinea pig in Nicky's small hands.

Drawn to the cozy scene, Sam went over and knelt down by Nicky. "Let me have a look."

Nicky held up the guinea pig. "He has long whiskers, Daddy!"

Sam stroked the little guy's side. "Yes, he sure does."

"Mine has whiskers, too," Rosie announced. "Pretty white ones!"

"Whiskers always match," Allison said. "Just as a purse should always match your shoes. Right, Rosie?"

"Right, Miss Allison!" Rosie said with a definitive nod that sent her dark curls bouncing.

Sam chuckled and regarded Allison, enjoying the sight of her tucked between the kids. She met his gaze over the twins' heads, grinning, her blue eyes sparkling. Sam smiled back, holding her gaze for one second, then two, then three. Awareness sparked through him, setting his pulse skyward, and he thought he could get lost in those eyes—

"Well, isn't this a touching little scene," a familiar voice said. "Looks like I got here just in time."

Sam looked left. And there, bearing down on the group, was Teresa, her eyes afire and her mouth pressed into a grim line.

Dread shot through him and he hoped she wouldn't make a scene. "Teresa," he said. "I...had no idea you'd be here." This kind of small-town activity wasn't exactly her style. He'd always come by himself in the past.

She slanted a narrow gaze toward Allison. "I thought I'd better come on down and see what's going on."

"We're going around to all the booths," Sam said truthfully. "The kids wanted to come to this one first."

"Mama!" Nicky said. "Look what I have. A guinea pig!"

With her gaze fixed on Allison, Teresa toddled over on her high black city-girl heels, which she wore with tight jeans and a black leather coat. She had an ugly hot-pink purse—designer, Sam was sure—hooked over one wrist. "I see that, honey." She flipped her long bottle-blond hair over her shoulder. "Looks like you guys are having a wonderful time." She patted Nicky on the head.

"You want to pet my guinea pig, Mommy?" Rosie asked. "I bet Miss Allison wouldn't mind."

Allison rose and smiled awkwardly. "Of course not." She gave the guinea pig back to

Chase, who'd stayed nearby to supervise the handling of the creatures. "I'm Allison True." With a small smile, she held out her hand to Teresa. "I own Happy Endings Bookstore."

Teresa looked at Allison's hand as if she'd been holding plutonium, but didn't offer her own. "I'm Teresa, Nicky and Rosie's mom."

After an uncomfortable moment, Allison dropped her hand. "I'm so glad to finally meet you," she said kindly. "The kids have told me all about you."

Sam had to give her credit. She sounded as if her words were true. But how could they be? Teresa was being a pill.

"I'm not into books, so I haven't been to Happy Endings." Teresa looked around. "In fact, I haven't shopped on Main Street at all. I think this whole SOM Committee thing is a complete waste of time."

"It's SOS, Teresa," Sam put in, his jaw tight.

She waved a French-manicured hand in the air. "Whatever."

"The plan is designed to help the town," Allison said succinctly. "But it will only work if the townspeople support it."

"Yes, well, Spense and I are...talking about moving, so Bygones isn't really my problem."

Sam mentally rolled his eyes. Man, Teresa had changed since he'd met her, into a woman he hardly recognized. He saw now that he'd had blinders on for a long time. Seeing the new Teresa—the one who'd materialized when she'd met Spense—made him sad for what he and the kids had lost.

But that ship had sailed, and Sam had to accept the facts, which wasn't hard when Teresa was acting so petty. "Was there something you wanted?" he asked in a level tone, trying to keep his patience, which was always a challenge with Teresa.

"Besides spending time with my kids?" she asked sharply.

"Yes, besides that," he ground out.

"Well, since you asked, I do have something I'd like to discuss with you." She paused and threw Allison a glare. "In private."

Uh-oh. His former wife was on the warpath, and he had a feeling he knew why; Teresa's pointed look at Allison told that story. "Right now?" Sam asked, frowning.

"I'm here, aren't I?" Teresa said, her voice dripping with annoyance.

Allison darted her eyes back and forth between him and Teresa, and then quickly piped in, "Um…I'd be happy to stay with the kids. Actually," she said, craning her neck, "I think Sweet Dreams is selling baked goods to raise money for the SOS Committee. How about I take these two little guinea-pig wranglers over there for a treat?"

Sam gave her a grateful look. Bless her kind, unselfish heart. "Thanks, that'd be great."

Teresa just sniffed.

Nicky handed his guinea pig back to Chase and then Allison took the twins' hands. "Let's go get a cupcake, all right?"

"Be sure and find some hand sanitizer before they eat," Teresa said. "Animals are so germy."

Sam cringed. "Teresa…"

"Well, they are," she said.

"On it," Allison said with a terse nod as she led the kids toward the opposite end of the room.

Sam turned to Teresa, his neck muscles tight. "Let's go somewhere else." He didn't want her making a fuss in public, and with Teresa, that was always a possibility.

"Fine," she said. "It's stuffy in here, anyway."

Now that she'd arrived, yes. But he'd keep that uncharitable thought to himself.

He went up the stairs leading from the basement into a hallway that led to the church vestibule. Teresa followed, her heels clickety-clacking on the wood floors, and he wondered how she managed the high, uncomfortable-looking shoes all the time. He remembered when she was happy in tennis shoes and comfy jeans. Those days were long gone, along with the Teresa he'd fallen in love with in college. Where had he gone wrong?

With that question ringing in his brain, he mentally geared himself up for the conversation to come. He knew the way Teresa rolled. Unfortunately. Her glare at Allison had spoken volumes. She was mad. And he was getting tired of her tantrums. Especially when they might be pointed at Allison.

When he reached the vestibule, he turned and said without preamble, "What's this all about, Teresa? Obviously you didn't come here for the festivities."

"You've got that right." She lifted her chin. "I'd heard that you and the kids have been spending a lot of time with Allison True, so I thought I'd better see for myself what was going on."

Bingo. "There's nothing 'going on,'" he said truthfully.

"Funny, it looked pretty cozy there when I walked in," she replied.

"We were holding *guinea pigs*. How is that cozy?" For the life of him, he didn't understand why she twisted things around like this.

"I heard you and Allison are dating," she added.

What? He blinked, incredulous and angry and fed up all at once. He sucked in a big breath, aiming for control. He'd need it with Teresa bending everything into kinks to suit her own purposes. "We are *not* dating—not that that's any of your concern."

"You have been spending time with her,

though." Teresa's brown eyes were sharp. "Amber Valois saw you and her playing at the park with the kids recently." Amber was Spense's sister, and Teresa's new best friend. All her other friends had faded into history when she'd cheated on Sam and dumped him.

He held on to his patience by a thread. "Yes, we took the kids to the park—for the kids. It was not a date." He could truthfully say he'd done everything possible to keep Allison safely in the friend category. "My conscience is clear."

Teresa crossed her arms over her middle. "So you're saying there is nothing romantic going on between you two."

"Yes, that's what I'm saying."

Doubt entered her eyes. "I'm not so sure men and women can be friends, that's all. I just assumed there had to be something romantic going on."

"That's your lens, Teresa, not mine." He swung around, his hands clenched at his sides. For his own self-respect—and to defend Allison—he had to call Teresa out on this. "My relationship with Allison is strictly for the kids. They love her, and she's wonderful with them. I would think you'd want them to spend time with people who are kind and giving and a positive influence, and I'll thank you to give me a bit more credit." It felt good to finally stand up to Teresa, to make himself heard.

Teresa paused. "It sounds like you like her."

"I do like her, Teresa, because she's nice to my kids. That's what this is about. I will always put the twins first. You know this about me, and frankly, I'm getting tired of you doubting my parenting skills. I have never given you a reason for that."

She sank into a bench next to the sanctuary doors, her shoulders bowed. Her purse clattered to the floor. "You're a good father, Sam. The best," she whispered.

He shook his head. "Then why do you always make me feel like a total failure?"

She hesitated. "I guess it makes me feel like less of a failure. Motherhood never came easily to me." Teresa looked confident on the outside, but inside she was a mishmash of insecurity. She'd had a tough childhood when her parents had been killed when she was six, and she'd been raised by an alcoholic aunt who'd never had time for her. She'd never dealt well with that burden.

"I know, and that first year was brutal. Sleepless nights. Endless crying from the kids." He shook his head ruefully. "And, boy, were we both exhausted."

"It went on and on."

"And it drove us apart rather than bringing us together."

"I needed an escape," Teresa said, sadness tingeing her voice. "I felt so…tied down. So inadequate."

"And that led you to Spense," Sam said carefully. Just the fact that he could utter those words in a normal tone showed him he'd made progress. What was the saying? What doesn't kill us makes us stronger?

"Yes. I wasn't looking for someone else," she said, her eyes now watery. "I really wasn't. I was just so overwhelmed…"

"I know." A heavy weight eased from Sam's shoulders.

"You fought harder than I did," she said,

tears brimming. "I'll always respect you for that."

"I did it for the kids."

She wiped her damp cheeks. "You've always been less selfish than me."

"Parenting is difficult, and it's not easy for me, either. But these are our children we're talking about. We have to do our best by them."

"Yes, I agree on that."

He had to ask a tough question, even though he might not like the answer. "Well, then, why have you been making noise about trying to get full custody?"

She shrugged. "I guess I was afraid Nicky and Rosie would somehow love me less if they had another mother figure in their lives."

Ah. There was that inherent insecurity of hers again; it colored everything Teresa did, and in the end, it had been instrumental in tearing their marriage apart. It was still wreaking havoc in his life. "You're their mother and always will be. No one can take your place."

"That's what Spense said."

Sam raised his eyebrows. For once, he and Spense agreed on something. "Well, maybe you should listen to him." Sam looked right at her, gearing up to get everything out on the table once and for all. He was tired of not knowing where he stood. He had to be honest or he'd always be unsure. "My lawyer advised me not to risk dating anyone in case you went for full custody, even though technically it shouldn't make a difference."

She took a shaky breath. "My insecurity brought out the worst in me."

Agreed. He bit his tongue and waited for her to finish. She had to make this decision on her own or it wouldn't mean anything.

Going on, she said, "I've seen how much the kids love you, and how excited they are when you come to pick them up. I really do want what's best for them, so I've decided I'm not going to push for full custody."

Relief loosened the muscles in his shoulders. "What about your plans to move?" he asked. He wanted all questions answered.

She rose and hiked her purse into the crook of her elbow. "Spense has accepted a job in Kansas City. I thought you and I could continue sharing custody—maybe a couple weeks at a time—until the kids go to kindergarten, and we can work that out then."

This news of a move wasn't surprising. Teresa had never been happy in such a small town. "I know it's time for you to really move on. I need to do the same. We both need new lives, and you'll never get the one you want if you stay here."

"Yes, that's true. I need to do this."

"I hope you find what you're looking for." It hadn't been him, and he had to accept that for good, even though this hadn't been the way he'd envisioned his life working out.

"Thank you." She straightened her shoulders. "Okay, I'll have my lawyer call yours regarding the change in the amount of time we each have the twins in the custody agreement."

"Great."

She gave him a small wave. "I'm going to go say goodbye to the kids."

"Bye," he said. "I'll be down in a minute."

She left, her steps softer on the plank

floors, and he was left alone, his thoughts swirling. She and Spense were leaving town. She wasn't going for full custody. *Thank You, God.*

Sam had stood up to Teresa once and for all. That felt great. He'd asserted himself to keep his self-respect. And to defend Allison, who'd only had good intentions with regards to the kids.

His thoughts swung to her. He needed to protect his heart; love was dangerous. Plus, he could be leaving town. Did he really want to take a dangerous inbound pass if he couldn't make a sure shot? Risky move. One that terrified him.

His gaze caught on the doors to the sanctuary right in front of him. He was, as Allison had said, in the Lord's house; strength awaited if he chose to ask for God's ear. Without pause, he opened the doors and stepped into the chapel, his eyes on the cross hanging above the altar. He sat in the last pew and a sense of calm came over him. It was good to be back here, good to be able to look to the Lord for guidance.

With that thought, he bowed his head and prayed. He had a feeling he was going to need all the help he could find in the days to come.

Chapter Thirteen

Allison took the kids around to all the booths, hoping Sam didn't mind that she was letting them eat the cupcakes they'd decorated at the Sweet Dreams booth. Honestly, with Teresa in the building, Allison was too nervous to deny them treats. Obviously Teresa was upset with Sam, and the razor-sharp look she'd thrown Allison had suggested Teresa wasn't happy with her, either.

Well, Allison thought as the kids made mini flower arrangements at the Love in Bloom booth, she had nothing to hide. She and Sam were just friends. That hadn't changed. Though the sizzling look they'd shared just before Teresa had arrived had felt unfriend-like for sure.

Still, a look was just a look. It was her actions with Sam that counted, and on that she was squeaky clean. Their relationship had been all about the kids, aboveboard at all times. She would always have their best interests in mind.

Teresa breezed up while they were watching some of the older kids carve pumpkins. The twins were eating their cupcakes, and Allison cringed when she realized their faces looked a mess, covered in cake crumbs and frosting.

"I was going to wipe their faces after they finished eating," she explained.

"Yeah, no use in trying to clean them up before they're done." Teresa hunkered down between the twins—a real feat in those heels—and put an arm around each of them. "Did you guys have fun?"

"Uh-huh," Nicky said, licking the frosting off his fingers. "She helped me with my cupcake."

"Me, too," Rosie added. "Miss Allison is so nice."

Teresa slanted a glance up at Allison. "That's what I hear."

Allison blinked but stayed silent. *What?*

"Well, my darlings," Teresa said, "I have to go. I will see you on Monday, all right?"

She hugged both kids, and then rose, her gaze on Allison.

Allison shifted from foot to foot.

Teresa hesitated, and then adjusted her hot-pink purse. "I...wanted to thank you for being so good to the twins."

Allison gulped. "You're welcome. They're great kids, and I like spending time with them."

"Sam's a good dad," Teresa said.

"Yes, he is." Allison hesitated. "He always wants what's best for Nicky and Rosie," she added.

"I know that." Teresa nodded, short and sweet. "My children are very lucky."

"Yes, they are," Allison agreed. Anyone would be lucky to have Sam in their life.

Teresa looked as if she wanted to say something, but instead she clamped her mouth shut, said goodbye and left, taking small steps as she walked to the stairs. Allison was sure she'd have those heels off pronto.

Allison breathed a sigh of relief—crisis averted, maybe?—even as she wondered what Teresa and Sam had talked about. She quickly curbed that interest. None of her business, really, though she was curious.

The twins finished their cupcakes and she grabbed a couple of paper towels at the bobbing-for-apples station and got them cleaned up, keeping an eye out for Sam. After they went back to the Fluff & Stuff booth to look at the gerbil habitat Chase had set up, she herded the twins to the Fixer-Upper booth.

She said hello to Coraline, who was there making the rounds, and Coraline smiled broadly as her gaze took in Allison and the twins. Allison smiled back, trying to look neutral. No sense in getting Coraline asking a lot of questions Allison couldn't answer.

She and the kids were hammering nails into boards with Gracie's help at the small workshop she and Patrick had set up at their booth when Sam arrived back on the scene.

"Well, it looks like we have a couple of budding carpenters on our hands," he said.

Allison noted that some of the lines on his face had relaxed. "And florists and cupcake decorators," Allison said, trying to tame her nerves. Sam didn't look upset. In fact, he looked calm and at ease. Good.

Nicky turned their way. "I had a choc-o-late one, and a banilla one."

"I just had banilla," Rosie announced. "With pink frosting."

Allison looked at Sam sheepishly. "I let them eat a lot." She picked up a small white bakery bag. "I made you one for later. I figured you for a chocolate guy."

He took the bag, the corners of his mouth turned up ever so slightly. "Why, thank you, baker Allison. I'll eat it later." His gaze fell on the kids. "They're having a great time."

"It doesn't get any better than cute animals, cupcakes and hammers, does it?"

"I don't think that stuff is the main draw here today."

She frowned. "What is? Food? Games? Fun?"

"You," he said, his brown eyes twinkling. "The twins love you."

Her heart turned over. "I love them, too, and it makes me happy to be around them." Maybe...that was because Sam was usually around when the kids were? She veered away from that thought. Nothing but trouble there. Besides, she'd love Nicky and Rosie with or without Sam.

Rosie dropped her hammer and came over. "Daddy, I want to go over there," she said, pointing right. "Miss Wilson says we can bod for apples."

Sam frowned. "Bod?"

"I think she means *bob* for apples," Allison clarified.

"Yeah, that," Rosie said. "Take me, Daddy, before all the apples are gone."

"Okay, sweetheart, we'll go." He glanced at Nicky, who was still pounding away on nails.

"I'll stay here with Nicky," Allison said. "You guys go and do some *bodding*."

"Great." With a smile, Sam started toward

the center of the room. But then he stopped and turned around. "Um, I was thinking maybe you'd like to come over for dinner and we can talk after the kids go to bed."

She did a double take. "I-is that a good idea?"

"Trust me, it's fine." He nodded, then mouthed, "We'll talk later, all right?"

"O…kay," she said in a strangled voice. Obviously something had changed. But what?

"Great. My famous macaroni and cheese is on the menu, so you won't want to miss that."

"You cook?"

"I open the blue box," he said with a sheepish grin.

"Even better," she replied, barely resisting the urge to press a hand to her chest. Clearly Sam had something on his mind. Something big if he was inviting her to dinner at his house. By tacit agreement she didn't push for details right now. But she trusted him implicitly, and if he wanted to talk, she'd talk.

Sam and Rosie went off to the bobbing-for-apples station and Allison tried to still her racing heart. She joined Nicky and hit some nails. Hard. There was nothing better than some aggressive hammer pounding to calm her nerves.

Good for now. But what would help her later, when she was alone with Sam, having a discussion about who-knew-what? It had to be big. She'd have to figure that out. Fast.

With Allison by his side, Sam tiptoed down the creaky stairs after they'd put the twins to bed together.

Allison giggled. "It's funny we're sneaking around your own house."

"It took us forty-five minutes and four stories to get them to sleep. I don't want to wake them up anytime soon." Though he'd loved having her help him get the kids settled. He'd missed having a partner on so many levels it wasn't even funny.

"Is it always this hard to get them to bed?" Allison asked when they reached the main level.

"No, not usually. But I think our piggyback race rematch got them worked up." By unspoken agreement, he'd made sure Allison and

Rosie won the race this time. "Or maybe it was our exciting game of Candyland."

"Yeah, they were pretty wound up after that."

"Not to mention their favorite person is here, and that is way more exciting than sleeping." He himself would stay up all night long if it meant getting to spend more time with Allison. Fighting the truth was hard. Impossible lately.

"You flatter me," she said, sinking onto the leather couch in the family room just off the kitchen.

"It's true," he replied, sitting next to her, instantly smelling the peachy scent she wore. He resisted the urge to move closer; he needed some semblance of control.

She turned those big blue eyes his way. "They sure had a good time today, didn't they?"

"The best. This is the first time they've been old enough to really appreciate the festival."

"I'm thinking there's a guinea pig in your future."

He laughed. "Not until they're old enough to take care of one."

"A gerbil, maybe?"

"Not that, either."

Allison chewed her bottom lip. "Sam, now that the kids are down, we need to have that talk."

"Yeah, I know." So far they'd dedicated the evening to the twins and hadn't been able to have any kind of private discussion. But he had to tell her about his and Teresa's conversation, for his own sake, and to ease her mind about being here. "Obviously, Teresa and I talked."

"Yes," Allison said, nodding mechanically. Clearly she was trying to keep a neutral demeanor. No surprise there. She didn't want to step on toes, and with Teresa's behavior, he couldn't blame Allison.

"Well, she thought we were dating."

Allison thinned her lips. "We've been very careful not to."

"Yes, we have, and I told her that we weren't dating."

"Good."

He turned and put his arm on the back of the couch. "I also asked her why she kept hanging the custody thing over my head."

"You did?" Allison whispered.

"Yes."

"Why?"

"Well, I realized that for us both to move on, I needed to confront her on all of it."

"You had good reasons," Allison said. "Nicky and Rosie."

"Exactly." He inclined his head.

"I think you did the right thing, Sam."

"Thanks." Her approval meant a lot to him; he respected her opinion. "I should also tell you her other news."

Allison raised her eyebrows.

"Teresa and Spense are moving to Kansas City."

"Oh, wow." A furrow formed above Allison's nose. "What about the twins?"

"We're going to continue sharing custody, with more time spent at a time with each of us. When the kids go to kindergarten, we'll review."

"Oh, Sam, that's great," Allison said. "They need their mother as much as they need you."

Of course, Allison would think that. She didn't have a malicious bone in her body.

"I appreciate your support." He took her hand in his. "It means a lot to me."

"So what does this mean, for, um, us?"

"I'm not sure, actually." He cleared his throat. "I find myself in a bit of a…dilemma." It was getting harder and harder to keep Allison at a safe emotional distance. He'd been fighting that since they met.

She toed off her flat shoes and tucked her legs up onto the couch, angling her body even more so she was closer and facing him. "Go on."

He noticed a stray tendril of hair floating above her ear and wanted to reach out and smooth it away. But he held back. "See, the thing is, I'm finding it hard to give in to the kids and spend time with you while also keeping things…impersonal."

"Yeah, I get that." Her eyes fluttered and she sagged closer, never breaking their gaze. "Impersonal is…hard."

His heart thundered. "Yes, impossible," he said, staring into her eyes, moving closer.

"What are we doing, Sam?" she breathed.

"Kissing?"

All she did was nod.

He should resist this, he hazily thought. But he'd battled his attraction to her for too long, and the fight had gone out of him, worn down by the wonderful person she was, by how lovingly she'd kissed his kids good-night and by how they'd both clung to her, clearly hating to see her go.

Without another rational thought he lowered his head and kissed her, soft and gentle. She kissed him back, and he lost track of time, lost everything but his connection to Allison.

Finally, she pulled away and laid her head on his shoulder. "Wow," she said. "That was...amazing."

He put his arm around her and pulled her closer. "Yes, it was." And it had been way too long since he'd kissed a woman, much less an all-around beautiful one like Allison.

She paused for a moment, resting her

hand on his chest, creating a pocket of tingly warmth under her fingers. Her cheeks flushed a pretty shade of pink, but she remained silent.

"What are you thinking?" he asked.

"That I'm glad the thing with Teresa has worked out."

A chill moved through him. "So…are you thinking that now…you want more?"

"Maybe." She regarded him. "What about you?"

"Honestly, I'm not sure."

She moved away. "You're still scared."

"Terrified."

"I'm scared, too. I learned at a very early age not to put too much stock in love."

"Your parents," he stated, his lips stiff.

"Yes." Her eyes glittered. "They withheld love, and it really wounded me."

"Just like my mom." The word *mom* was bitter on his lips; if anyone was less deserving of that title, it was Doris Franklin.

"Exactly, so you know what it's like when someone who should love you doesn't." She looked down and rubbed the surface of her jeans. "I've never felt worthy of love, so it's very difficult for me to admit I even want it."

His heart cracked. "You deserve it," he said. "More than anyone I've ever known."

She gazed at him, her eyes pools of blue. "But you don't?"

He froze. "It's not so much that I don't think I deserve it. It's more that I'm not sure I can take the risk."

"You kissed me," she whispered.

"Yes, I did. Maybe I shouldn't have." He'd let himself get carried away with all the good things about Allison. That had been a mistake. Man, he was making a mess of this.

She blinked, nodding, her jaw taut. "Then I guess we're done here." She rose.

He started to get up.

Holding out a hand, she said, "No, don't. I'll see myself out."

"Allison—"

"Just don't say anything," she said. "This is probably best. I have other important things on my plate right now, and I wasn't planning on a romance."

"The bookstore."

"Yes. I have to make it work, Sam. It's so important to me, and the town. That has to come first in my life."

"I respect that." What else could he say? Her dedication was one of the things he liked most about her.

"Good." She picked up her purse. "I'll see you around."

He just nodded.

And then she walked out, the front door clunked closed and he sat there alone, his arms empty, his heart cracking around the edges. But he was safe, and right now, that was what mattered most.

Chapter Fourteen

Allison sat in a booth at the Cozy Cup Café, trying desperately to listen as all the shop owners reported on the progress of their businesses to date.

It was Josh Smith's turn to host the Shopkeepers' Society meeting, which rotated between SOS businesses every month. So he was there, as was Coraline, Lily, Patrick, Chase and Melissa.

Allison had left Viv in charge of Happy Endings to go to the meeting. She should be paying attention. But, as usual lately, she was having a hard time thinking about anything but how Sam had pulled away three nights ago. Though he'd probably done the smart thing, all things considered, she still felt sad. Neither one of them was ready to make any kind of commitment. Sam might be leaving Bygones soon. She had to stay. And both of them had fences around their hearts. Those things meant she needed to keep herself under strict control.

"Allison, dear, what do you think of that idea?"

Coraline's voice jerked Allison back to reality. "Wh-what?" she stammered, her cheeks flaming.

Coraline gave her an indulgent smile. "We were talking about the idea of having a sidewalk Christmas sale in December."

"Oh." Allison shifted in her seat. "Um, well, I think that sounds like a great idea."

"Wonderful." Coraline beamed. "So we're all in agreement."

Chase held up a rigid hand. "I wanted to mention that I'd be happy to be in charge of stringing some of the lights on Main Street." Chase was a good guy—he'd been really gentle with Nicky and Rosie when they'd held the guinea pigs at the Harvest Festival—but to Allison he often seemed a bit tense.

"I'll help with that, too," Patrick said as he unfolded his tall body from the small chair across from Allison. "I have the ladders we'll need." Patrick was patient and kind, and a bit on the quiet side. He and Gracie Wilson planned a spring wedding next year.

Lily adjusted the tortoiseshell glasses perched on her nose. "I'm sure Tate would want to help with that."

"I'll help, too," Melissa added as she smoothed some of her long red hair back behind her ear. She, too, was on the tall side, and had a wellspring of energy that Allison envied. She and her fiancé, Brian, were engaged to be married in January. Seemed the love bug had bitten quite a few of the Main Street shopkeepers.

"Excellent," Coraline said, her blue eyes shining.

Chase raised a hand. "I'd like to address some of the acts of vandalism that have occurred lately."

Coraline looked down at the papers neatly

stacked on the table in front of her. "Yes, I have that on my list of things to discuss."

Though her store hadn't been vandalized, Allison had heard that some small things had gone missing from some of the stores lately, some picnic tables had been turned over at the Everything and some windows had been broken around town.

"Thankfully, Brian's tools were returned," Melissa said. Allison had heard that Melissa's fiancé's mechanics tools had been stolen from his shop on the outskirts of town. "He was really steaming about that."

"Of course he was," Patrick said. "Those tools were expensive. Does Chief Sheridan have any leads?"

Coraline shook her head. "Not yet."

"I think it's odd that someone would do something like that," Josh commented. "We're all working so hard to bring the town back to save the schools and the police force. Why would someone want to jeopardize that?"

There were murmurs of agreement.

"Well, we all know not everybody is all

that gung-ho on the SOS Committee's plan," Chase said. "A lot of people in town questioned the wisdom of bringing in newcomers to run the Main Street businesses rather than awarding the businesses to locals."

"But to deface property and steal?" Allison said. "That just seems foolish."

"Well, with the reduced police force, maybe they're just crimes of opportunity," Patrick remarked.

"Still, it's weird," Lily commented. "Particularly since the thief brought the stolen items back."

"We'll all just have to be extra vigilant, then." Coraline adjusted her glasses. "Remember to lock your doors and be on the lookout for strangers, or anything else that seems out of place."

"Any word on who our mysterious benefactor is?" Melissa asked, shifting gears.

"Yeah." Lily leaned forward. "It would be nice to get his take on this."

"Or hers," Allison interjected. It wasn't even known if the mysterious benefactor was a man or a woman.

"No, not yet," Coraline replied. "The bene-factor's identity is still unknown."

"I still think it's strange that he—or she—is staying anonymous," Patrick said. "Although, if the plan fails—which I'm not saying it will, just speculating how someone else might feel—it might be a lot easier to cut bait if no one knows their identity."

"The plan is solid," Chase said. "It will work, so no need for bait cutting."

Lily said, "Main Street is beautiful and our businesses are doing reasonably well so far."

"Even so, many people in town are still skeptical," Melissa said. "Inez Sheridan was just in to order a cake for her daughter's birth-day, and she told me that no one in her bridge club is holding out much hope that the SOS Committee's plan to save the town will actu-ally work." Allison's heart sank. What would Sam do if budget cuts caused him to lose his job? Would he really have to leave town? She clenched her hands in her lap.

"We have to hold out hope," Patrick coun-seled.

"People change," Chase added.

"All the time." Coraline took off her glasses. "We have to have faith, because without faith we have nothing. I suggest we all pray about this."

Allison nodded along with everyone else.

With that, Coraline adjourned the meeting and everyone rose. Allison remained seated for a moment, still a bit shocked by her dramatic reaction to the prospect of Sam and the twins possibly leaving town. She took a swig of coffee. Truth be told, she'd be devastated if the Franklins left Bygones. Wrecked, actually. Totally wrecked.

What did that mean?

That bombshell was set aside when she spied Robert Randall arriving. Coraline went over and talked to him as he ordered from Josh. They were about the same age, and they looked good together, him tall, her petite, with their matchy-matchy gray hair. Was there something between them, a romance, maybe? Were they a...couple?

A couple. Able to lean on and support each other through good and bad, up and down, high and low and everything in between. What would that be like?

With a wistful smile Allison turned, only to observe Brian Montclair arrive and sweep his fiancée, Melissa, into his arms and plant a huge kiss on her lips. They had only been engaged a short time and were so clearly deeply in love it made Allison's heart clench.

She ripped her gaze from the happy couple. She hated feeling so sappy. She had no time or reason for sappiness. Sam had made his feelings clear.

Lily stopped next to her, a cup of coffee in hand. "They look ecstatically happy, don't they?"

"They sure do." Allison regarded Lily. "You are, too, aren't you?"

Lily blushed. "Oh, yes. Tate's…wonderful." She grinned. "And so is Isabella."

"Yes, you're a wife and a mother now. That must be amazing."

"I couldn't love Isabella more if she were my own child." Lily looked intently at Allison. "Haven't you been spending some time with Sam Franklin and his twins?"

"Um…yes."

"Are you two dating?"

"Absolutely not."

"But you like him?"

"Yes, I do," Allison said truthfully.

"I sense a 'but' in there," Lily said with a raised eyebrow.

"But…I don't want to fall in love right now. I have to focus on the bookstore." Sam didn't want love, either.

"Hey, I didn't plan to fall in love."

"Why not?" Allison asked, unable to help herself. She needed a shoulder, someone to commiserate with, and Lily seemed like the perfect sounding board.

"Tate didn't want more kids and I did." Lily dropped her voice. "But then he said he couldn't live without me, and I was toast."

"How romantic," Allison said, a tad bit envious of Lily. She had what she wanted, what would make her happy. And Allison had… Happy Endings. Why didn't that seem like enough anymore?

Horrified, she shoved that thought away. Happy Endings had to be enough. "Any regrets?" Allison doubted it, if the look of pure bliss on Lily's face was any indication, but she had to ask. It seemed important to get a balanced story.

Lily smiled and her eyes sparkled with happiness. "None whatsoever. I can't imagine not having him and Isabella in my life."

Allison's chest tightened. "If the SOS plan doesn't pan out, Sam will have to take a job away from Bygones," she blurted.

"Oh, no," Lily said. "How do you feel about him possibly leaving?"

"Terrible," Allison said honestly.

"Sounds like your heart is telling you something."

"Maybe." She let out a breath. "But I'd be taking a big risk by putting my heart on the line."

"Big risk, big reward," Lily said.

"Or, big risk, get hurt." And the love that had been denied to Allison earlier in her life upped the stakes even more. Putting her heart in danger was a huge leap for her.

She just wasn't sure she could risk everything—her heart, her dreams for Happy Endings—for something so uncertain. Especially now that Sam had made his wishes plain.

"I'm going to pick up the bouquet from Love in Bloom." Allison had been working on the weekly book order and other administrative stuff since 6:00 a.m. and needed some fresh air and sunshine. Desperately. She probably looked more like a mole than a person at this point. Not a pretty thought.

Viv looked at her from the laptop Allison kept on the front counter. "Good idea. You've been cooped up in here all morning. Why don't you take a walk, maybe get some coffee? I'm going to keep working on the holiday flyers we designed." She squinted at the screen. "I'm not liking the border width."

"Sounds great." Allison nodded to the counter. "Mr. Fibley's order is right there if he comes in. He's been anxiously waiting for his philately books to arrive."

"Got it," Viv said, pointing to the bag. "Fibley's philately books." She grinned. "Wow. That's a tongue twister!"

Allison laughed. "Yes, it is." With a wave

she stepped out onto the sidewalk, breathed deep and took in the clear blue sky, stretching the kinks out of her back. Ah. Better.

Deciding to take Viv's advice—coffee sounded wonderful—she turned left and headed past Love in Bloom and Sweet Dreams. As she crossed Bronson Avenue, she waved to Miss Mars, who was sweeping the sidewalk out in front of the This 'N' That. Danny Wilbur, Kenneth Wilbur's teenage son, drove by in the tan-and-brown minivan he used to help Lily with flower deliveries. Allison waved to him, too, remembering that she'd promised Kenneth she'd research books on Alzheimer's since his mother, Ann, suffered from the disease and the whole family was dealing with it. She made a mental note to do that when she got back to the store.

Just as Allison arrived at the Cozy Cup, Whitney Leigh crossed the street from city hall. Her blond hair, which she always wore scraped back into a tight bun, glowed bright in the late-morning sun. She had a laptop case slung over one shoulder and, as usual, wore a severely cut black skirt and matching jacket.

"Good morning, Allison." Whitney looked at her watch. "Although, it's almost afternoon."

"Good morning, Whitney."

"How's the bookstore doing?" Whitney had interviewed her a few months ago for a feature in the *Bygones Gazette,* and Allison knew she was notoriously intent on discovering the identity of the mysterious Main Street benefactor.

"Well enough," Allison said, opening the door and holding it for Whitney. She was still walking a thin line between black and red, but she wouldn't let Whitney know that. "Story Time is a big hit, and the teen creative-writing workshops are going well."

Whitney went through the door. "Thanks. Good to hear Happy Endings is cooking along."

Allison followed her in, immediately noticing the rich scent of coffee that permeated the air in the café. "Any news on the benefactor?"

"No, not yet," Whitney said. "But I'm not giving up until I discover the truth."

"Well, good luck," Allison replied. If anyone could figure out that mystery it was Whitney; she had an investigative streak a mile wide, from what Allison could tell.

Whitney plopped herself down at one of the small tables near the front. "Thank you." She flopped the laptop case onto the table and began unzipping it.

Allison made her way to the counter to order.

"Good morning," Josh said. "What looks good?"

"I think I just need a plain old cup of black coffee." As in liquid caffeine. "To go, if you don't mind."

"Been working hard?" Josh asked as he grabbed a paper cup. "You looked a little tired at the Shopkeepers' Society meeting yesterday."

"Yeah, I was up late last night working, and up before the crack of dawn." And she'd lain awake thinking about Sam, so sleep had been elusive. She missed him, and the twins, when they weren't together. And she had no clue what to do about her feelings for him.

"Sounds like you're keeping killer hours." Josh filled the cup with coffee.

"Yeah, I am. Running a business is a lot of work."

He put the cup of steaming coffee on the counter and then pressed on a plastic sipper lid. "Is that inventory-control software working okay?"

"Oh, yes, I got that to work after you came and helped." She picked up the cup and inhaled the coffee-scented steam. "Thank you so much."

"Anytime. I love working with computers, so I don't mind at all."

She paid for the coffee and contemplated sitting down for a few minutes to enjoy it. But there was work to be done, so with a longing glance she bypassed all the glass-topped tables and headed toward the door. Helen Langston came in and said a stiff hello on her way to the front counter, her chin held at an imperious angle. Allison returned the greeting, shaking her head at Helen's stand-offish demeanor.

Then Allison left the café and slowly walked the scant block back to Happy Endings so as to enjoy the day—and her coffee. This was the only break she'd have today.

She crossed back over Bronson Avenue, mentally going over her extensive to-do list. Research Alzheimer's. Complete the weekly book order. Get started on her holiday marketing plan. The list was endless.

Just then, she spied a familiar tall figure across the street. Sam. On the sidewalk with Miss Mars in front of the This 'N' That. Allison's heart rate did its little Sam dance, the one that had butterflies flitting around in her tummy.

Without much thought she veered left and crossed Main Street. "Hey," she said when she arrived at the This 'N' That. "Whatcha doing?"

"This dear man came over to help me move some of my displays around," Miss Mars said, gesturing with a crooked hand to some rusty lawn furniture on the sidewalk. "Isn't that lovely?"

"Yes, that's right," Sam replied. "It's my planning period, so I was on my way to the Cozy Cup for some coffee and I saw Miss Mars here trying to move this stuff by herself. I felt obligated to offer my assistance." The school was just a few blocks away.

"As long as I have you here," Miss Mars said to Sam, "would you mind coming in and bringing that furniture with you?" she asked, pointing to the lawn furniture, which was fifty years old if it was a day. "And, if you could be so kind, could you also move some heavy boxes for me?" She looked up, squinting. "My, it's quite warm for October. I think I'll go in and wait for you there, my dear."

"Whatever you need, Miss Mars," Sam said, rolling his sleeves up. "Your wish is my command."

"Excellent." Miss Mars looked up at Sam, who undoubtedly stood a foot taller than she. "I always liked you, Sam, and now I know why." She turned her sharp gaze to Allison.

"I hope you realize what a splendid young man you have here."

Allison was incapable of responding. So she just nodded.

Miss Mars went on, "You're a very blessed woman, you know. You need to hold on to this one, if you ask me. Which you didn't. But I'm still telling you. I'm old, so I just tell it like I see it whether anybody really wants to hear it or not." With that proclamation, she turned and went inside, shuffling along, her snow-white head bent.

Allison watched her go, her jaw slack, her lips parted.

"You look like you're about to have kittens," Sam said, a smile in his voice.

Undoubtedly. And puppies and piglets. A regular farmyard, right here in the middle of Main Street. Miss Mars's words echoed in her brain.

You need to hold on to this one, if you ask me.

Someone called her name from her left. She looked over and saw Viv across the street, standing in front of Happy Endings, waving her arms.

"Mr. Fibley says you ordered the wrong book," Viv called. "Can you come over here and look into it?"

Allison waved back. "I'll be right there." She turned her attention to Sam. "Business calls. Mr. Fibley is very picky about his stamp-collecting books."

"Go. You're needed." Sam looked at his watch. "Oh, wow. Me, too. I only have twenty minutes until my next class starts, so I have to get moving if I want to help Miss Mars and get my coffee. I need some caffeine."

"You haven't been sleeping well?" she ventured.

"Nope." He caught her gaze and held it. "I've had a lot on my mind."

"Me, too," she whispered, unable to look away.

"Sam?" Miss Mars called. "Are you going to come help me or keep making goo-goo eyes at Miss True?"

The words had Allison jerking her gaze away, her cheeks heating. "With that, I think

I'll just move along and take care of Mr. Fibley," she said, pointing left.

"Your store is over there," Sam said with a crooked grin, pointing to *his* left.

She looked around. "Oh. You're right." Now her cheeks were on fire. He had her so discombobulated she didn't know which way was up. Or left or right. "Uh…I'm just going to leave now, before I get any more flustered."

"Okay. Me, too." He turned to go into the This 'N' That, then stopped and looked back at her. "The kids miss you."

Her insides twisted. "I miss them, too." And him, also. Would that ever change? Probably not.

"Maybe I'll bring them to Story Time soon."

"Yes, do." Though she and Sam had insurmountable walls up between them, she wouldn't cut the twins out of her life. "I'll pick out some special stories for them."

"They'd love that." He held up a hand. "Bye."

"Bye."

She watched him walk away and then hustled across the street to Mr. Fibley, trying not to feel her heart pushing in vain against the wall around it.

Chapter Fifteen

The day after Allison saw Sam at the This 'N' That she was busy all day long and had nary a free moment to think about their conversation. Maybe that was a good thing. She had to keep her attention on realistic endeavors.

Kenneth Wilbur came in to order some of the books on Alzheimer's she'd suggested, and Pastor Garman stopped by to browse the religion section, and the pet section, too, telling her his family was considering getting a dog and he needed a book on dog breeds. A stream of other customers came and went, and sales were steady. She also spent a few hours working on the holiday marketing plan in her office while Viv manned the front.

At about seven-thirty in the evening, Allison was still working, just about ready to fling her computer out the window onto Main Street. Her email account wasn't working, and she could not for the life of her fix it.

A headache loomed, right between her eyes.

A knock on the front door almost had her jumping out of her skin. Who could possibly be here at this hour? Main Street was normally dead at this time, especially during the week. All the businesses were closed.

She got up and her back twinged—ouch!—obviously mad at her being hunched over the computer for the past few hours. She stretched it out as she walked, wincing, wondering if she had any aspirin in her purse. This job's long hours were killing her physically. She needed a break, but she wasn't going to get one anytime soon. She'd deal. For Happy Endings.

When she got to the door, she peeked through the shut blinds.

Her breath caught. Sam stood there, waiting. Why was he here?

She opened the door. "Sam. I wasn't…um, expecting you."

"I know. I hope you don't mind that I stopped by. I took the kids to Teresa's and saw the light on here, so…" He shrugged. "Here I am."

She stepped back, her knees shaky. "Come on in. So the kids are okay?"

He entered. "They're fine."

She swung the door shut and locked it. "Oh, good."

His gaze roamed over her. One eyebrow crept up. "Nice outfit."

"Oh, thanks." As soon as the store had closed, she'd changed into pink fleece pants and a blue sweatshirt, and she had pulled her hair back in a haphazard ponytail. "It's going to be a long night, and I wanted to be comfortable."

"You look adorable," he said, smiling.

She swallowed and made a show of looking him over. "Well, so do you—just like the basketball coach you are." In her mind, his well-fitting black athletic pants and zippered top were just as attractive as any suit and tie. Maybe because that was Sam at heart—a coach—and she loved that part of him.

He roamed his gaze over her. "Exhausted?"

"Yep," she said, stretching. "My back isn't happy with me."

Lines formed above his nose. "You're spending too much time at your desk, I take it?"

"Probably." She shrugged. "Comes with the territory."

He studied her for a couple seconds, his eyes slightly narrowed. "Well, Miss True, then it's a good thing I stopped by."

She frowned.

"I'm taking you away for a break."

"What?" She shook her head. "No. I have to work."

"You can take a small breather," he said, taking her by the arm. "I'm a coach, well versed in how to pace oneself, and I insist you get out and stretch your legs."

She dug in her heels. "Sam, I have so much to do—"

"You'll get it done faster and more efficiently if you take care of yourself. Just listen to the coach, all right?"

She reluctantly let him pull her along. "Wh-where are we going? It's dark."

"I know my way around in the dark." He unlocked the door, opened it and propelled her through. "We used to run around at night all the time when we were growing up."

"We used to pretend we were secret agents," she said with a chuckle. "You were Boris and I was Natasha."

"You and Lori used to fight over who got to be Natasha."

"Ha. Yeah. I remember that." At that point she'd just liked Sam as another kid who was fun to play with. Funny how that had changed.

He went left, taking her with him. "Let's go to Bronson Park."

"You're not letting me out of this, are you?" She made herself sound a bit peeved, but she actually liked that he wanted to take care of her. No one had done that, well, ever. She'd always had to look out for herself.

"Nope." He tightened his arm around her. "So just go with it. You're working yourself ragged."

She relaxed just a bit. "I have to."

"I know, and I admire you for that. Hugely. You're committed to the bookstore, for good reason. But you aren't doing yourself any favors by abusing yourself."

His concern made her feel great. She wished it didn't.

When they reached Sweet Dreams, they went left at Bronson Avenue. Darkness had fallen, but the streetlights were still on, casting a dull light onto the street. The town was silent, save for the sound of a dog barking somewhere in the distance. Like most small towns, Bygones rolled up early. Luckily, it was a mild night, with just a small breeze to clear the cobwebs from her head.

Allison consciously let herself relax. She might as well go along with him. And she did need a break. Her brain felt like mush, and her body was complaining. And who better than to play hooky with than Sam?

Oh, wow. She shouldn't go there. This was just a break. Nothing more.

They walked the rest of the way in silence, and Allison's tummy came alive with butterflies. Soon they stood at the edge of the park. Sam looked around. "Let's go sit on the bench by the duck pond."

The park was shrouded in darkness, but Sam moved confidently to the bench on the far side of the pond. At this hour, the park was deserted, and no quacks sounded from the reeds on the right side of the pond. Even the ducks, it seemed, were sleeping.

She and Sam were alone. Her heartbeat went wild.

Without a word, Sam sat, drawing her down beside him. They sat in silence for a few beats of time, and then Sam's voice came out of the darkness.

"I've been thinking about you a lot."

She wanted to say she'd been thinking about him, too. But what good would that do? "Really?"

"Yes, really. That kiss has been on my mind for sure."

"Yeah, me, too," she replied in all honesty. So much for keeping things under wraps.

He turned. "I'd like to do it again."

She swallowed, trying to still her breathing. "Me, too. But…"

"But what?"

"I don't think we should," she said in a shaky voice. "You're not ready for a romance, and I…"

"You're not the kind of person to be trifled with."

"Same goes for you," she said. "Neither one of us should move forward unless we're absolutely sure."

He stayed quiet. "Of course, you're right."

"I wish I weren't."

He touched her hand and warmth tingled all the way up to her heart. "Me, too."

She made herself be pragmatic, and not grab his hand. "Well, then, looks like we've worked that out."

His jaw tightened.

"Have we really, Sam?"

"I'm scared to move forward."

"I understand," she said. And she did. So

well it hurt. "You have to figure that out for yourself."

All he did was nod, but uncertainty shone in his eyes.

She waited for a moment, waiting for more. Hoping…

He remained silent.

Message received. The truth hurt, but was needed. She stood, keeping her back rigid. Strong. "I need to get back to work." Thankfully, she had that.

He rose. "I'll walk you there."

"Okay," she said as she turned and headed toward Main Street.

After a bit of silence, he said, "Allison, I wish things were different."

"Wishing isn't enough."

Another pause. "Yes, I guess you're right," he replied. "After what happened with Teresa, I should know that by now."

"So should I," Allison said. She was through wishing for what could never be, what Sam couldn't allow. Even though that meant they would never have a chance.

* * *

The day after she'd gone to the park with Sam, Allison looked up from the front counter of Happy Endings and almost fainted.

Mom.

Allison stood, frozen in shock, as her mom came forward.

"You look surprised," her mother said.

"I…I am," Allison said. "You've never come in. And…you never leave the farm during the day." As in, ever. Not even for her kids' sporting events or graduations.

"I know, but, well, I needed some things from the Fixer-Upper, so I thought I'd stop by and see what you've been working so hard on. Amy's talked of nothing else since the store opened."

Allison blinked. *Thank you, sis.* "Um… well, great." She gestured around, feeling surreal. "This is my store."

Mom cast her gaze about, nodding. "Very nice. I love the shelves."

"I made them myself," Allison said proudly.

Her mother's eyebrows rose. "Really? I'm impressed."

Allison almost swooned again. Praise from her mom had been almost nonexistent. "I also did all the painting and decorating, too."

"Wow. You've worked hard. It's really nice. I especially like the color you chose for the walls."

Allison furrowed her brow. "Mom, while I appreciate the praise about my color choices, I doubt you came here to talk about paint."

Vera nodded. "Yes, you're right."

"What's on your mind?" Allison asked, steeling herself for whatever her mom had to say.

"After I saw you at the grocery store the other day, I got to thinking, and thought I should come by and clear some things up."

"What things?"

Mom sighed. "You obviously believe your father and I think you're going to fail."

All Allison could manage was a terse nod.

"Yes, well, that isn't really accurate."

"But...that's what you said."

"I know, but the truth is, we know how much hard work goes into running a business, how much it can take from a person."

"You said some of this at the grocery store."

"Yes, I did, but I clammed up and shouldn't have."

"You threw out the 'perhaps' code."

"Guilty," Mom said sheepishly. "I've never been good at discussing difficult things, and your father is even worse at it. That's just the way we were raised."

"So…?" Allison wasn't sure where this was going.

"The thing is, we know too well how much work's involved in what you're doing." Mom shoved her hands into her jeans' pockets. "We look back on the choices we made to run our own business, and we have some regrets."

Allison frowned. "You do?"

"For sure. We know how much we missed with you girls because of the farm."

"You missed everything," Allison said.

"I know. Amanda and Amy have been very vocal about us missing so much, and…Amy actually threatened to run away the other day."

Allison dropped her jaw. "But she didn't?"

"No, she just threatened."

"She's always been the one most likely to rock the boat."

"Yes, she has. And maybe that's a good thing. After that incident, I finally realized that they had a point. And that made me realize we don't want the same lifestyle for you."

Words froze in Allison's mouth. Unbelievable. In a good way.

"I can see you're stunned again," her mom said with a quirk of her mouth.

"Yeah." Allison pressed a hand to her forehead. "I wish you'd just told me this from the beginning."

"We should have, but you know what they say about hindsight."

"Twenty-twenty."

"I hope it's not too late." Mom shook her head. "In reality, I'm really proud of you for going for what you want with this store and for doing more than just wishing for things to fall in your lap. You really took a risk and it looks like it's going to turn out good."

"Wow. I'm not sure what to say," Allison replied. "I didn't expect this." Honestly, she would have been less surprised if it had snowed in July.

"You don't have to say anything. Just think about what I said, all right?"

"All right."

Mom stepped forward and pulled Allison into an awkward hug. "Thank you for hearing me out." She pulled back. "You've done a wonderful job here. Maybe you could come out for dinner someday. Amanda has become quite the cook."

Allison's eyes burned. "I'd like that, too."

Her mom turned and exited the shop, and Allison was left standing there feeling as if her world had started spinning the other way. Who would have thought her parents would come around after all these years of putting work before their family? She made a mental note to thank her sisters for calling their parents out on what was going on. They'd done what Allison had never had the courage to do.

One thing her mom had said stood out. *I'm really proud of you for going for what you want with this store and for doing more than just wishing for things to fall in your lap.*

There was that word again: wishing. Allison had brought up wishing last night with Sam, had said that wishing wasn't enough to make things come true. Her mom had just said the same thing. Suddenly, Allison realized that she'd been simply *wishing* for Sam to love her. But she hadn't done anything about it from her end.

She sagged against the counter.

The truth was, Sam made her feel happy, safe and cared for. When she was with him, she couldn't imagine not being with him. Nothing made her happier.

And the twins, bless their little souls, filled her heart with pure love, and she wanted to protect them and cherish them and watch them grow.

She wanted to be their mom.

A hot chill swept up her spine. She was in love with the Franklin family. All of them. And no matter how much she tried to fight the feeling, it was useless to try to deny how she felt.

And Sam was at the center of all of it.

She was in love with Sam and she had to

stop wishing for him to move forward. She had to take control of her future with him. And that meant she had to lay her heart on the line.

She had to tell him she loved him, or she'd regret it forever.

"Class dismissed," Sam announced right after the final bell rang. "Don't forget, people, the worksheets for chapter four are due on Monday, and there'll be a pop quiz sometime next week."

A collective groan sounded.

"I know, I know. I'm an ogre." Sam waved. "Have a good weekend."

The kids in his Algebra One class filed out of the classroom, talking amongst themselves, clearly eager for the weekend to start.

Johnny Tucker, a short skinny kid with glasses, stopped at Sam's desk.

Sam straightened some papers. "What can I do for you, Johnny?"

"I'm just not getting this stuff, Mr. Franklin." He swung a huge backpack onto his shoulder. "Any ideas about how I can get a clue?"

Sam wasn't surprised. Johnny's grades had fallen when they'd started chapter two and hadn't improved since. "I'd be happy to give you some extra help at lunchtime next week." Sam held after-school tutoring two days a week, but he knew Johnny's mom had gone back to work to help make ends meet since Randall Manufacturing had closed and Johnny's dad had lost his job. That meant Johnny had to go home and babysit his younger brothers every afternoon after school.

"You would?" Johnny's narrow shoulders sagged. "That'd be great."

"Sure." Sam stood. "Just come by on Monday with your lunch and we'll go over the material then. In the meantime, do your best on the worksheets, and maybe read over the chapter on the weekend."

"Thanks, Mr. Franklin," Johnny said. "I really appreciate it."

Sam squeezed Johnny's shoulder. "I know you do. And that's what I'm here for, so don't hesitate to let me know when you need extra help."

Johnny agreed and left, and a feeling of satisfaction spread through Sam. For some people, math wasn't the most thrilling subject—some found it boring, actually. But not Sam. He had always loved the logic inherent in mathematics and loved when kids made the connection and saw that. With his help, Johnny could get back on track, and Sam would rest well knowing he had made a difference.

Which was exactly why he'd become a teacher. What would he do if he lost his job? He couldn't imagine he'd be happy doing anything else. He hoped it wouldn't come to that.

He loved his job here.

Knowing he had a few minutes before he left to take the kids to Story Time, he sat down to check his email so he could get organized to send out notices about the upcoming parent-teacher conferences he had scheduled.

As the program lumbered along—old, slow computer—his thoughts turned to Allison.

He and the kids had spent some time with her since the night he'd kissed her after the harvest festival, and he had to admit, their relationship had taken on a new dimension. And yesterday, when he'd seen her in front of Miss Mars's store? Well, he'd wanted to take Allison in his arms and convince her to take Miss Mars's advice. But Allison was cautious, and he understood why. They'd grown closer over the past week, despite their better judgment.

And last night? He'd sought her out at the bookstore because he hadn't been able to stay away and hadn't had the willpower to fight seeing her. She'd needed a break, clearly, and he'd had a big need to take care of her, to wipe away the shadows evident beneath her eyes.

One thing was clear: she was working her way into his heart, and he wasn't sure how to stop it.

His computer pinged, indicating he had a new email, drawing his attention away from his feelings for Allison and the predicament they presented. He clicked on his in-box and saw that he'd received a message from Lakeland City School District.

With a shaky hand he double clicked and read the short email. The school district in Florida was extending him a job offer, to start in the new year!

Wow. He sat back in his chair. This had happened faster than he'd anticipated; he'd applied as backup, and had figured the online video interview was just an in-case procedure on the district's part. But he hadn't expected anything much to come of any of it, given the dearth of teaching jobs due to the economy and the fact that they were midway through the school year. But…here was a job. There for the taking. This was the answer to his prayers.

He rubbed his eyes, troubled. While this was positive news, the truth was that he didn't want another job. He loved the one he had, in the town he loved, with the students he'd bonded with. Students like Johnny and Rory and Scott and so many others. He loved walking down the street and having people ask him about the team, showing interest in his boys. Just the thought of leaving Bygones made his stomach pitch.

Plus…Allison was here, and would be for the foreseeable future. She loved her job and had worked herself weary for the bookstore, for Bygones. For *him,* and for everybody else in town whose job was at risk. Her priorities were here. His might not be. Who knew? Nobody did, not until it became clear if the SOS Committee's plan would work and the schools would be safe.

He put his head in his hands. He had no answers, except that an already complicated situation had just become even more complex.

A job awaited, a sure thing, his livelihood restored, his family secure. Could he really turn that down? He didn't know.

"Sam, is everything all right?"

Sam looked up. Coraline stood in the doorway to his classroom, holding a clipboard. "Oh, hi, Coraline."

She came into the room. She wore a bright blue skirt and jacket that was the same color as her eyes, along with sensible, low-heeled black shoes and tasteful gold-tone jewelry. "You look distressed."

He sighed. "Well, I am dealing with a bit of a dilemma."

"Dare I say it has something to do with Miss True?" Coraline asked, stopping in front of his desk.

He nodded. "It might."

"You two have grown close, haven't you?"

His stomach clenched. "You could say that." Out of respect for Allison, he wouldn't go into detail.

Coraline set the clipboard down. "And... that's causing you to question your path?"

"Yes."

"Well, would you like my advice?"

"Would it matter if I said no?" he asked with a small smile.

She laughed. "Probably not."

"Then fire away." He trusted Coraline and respected her judgment, and he needed all the help he could get right now.

"I think you should pray about this, Sam. God will show you the way."

"I have been praying."

"But you're still doubtful?"

"Yes. I feel like I'm being pulled in too many ways." He wouldn't mention the job offer right now; he needed time to think about it before he shared his news with anyone, most especially his boss.

"Well, keep praying, and have faith in God's counsel."

"I'll do my best."

"Good." She picked up her clipboard. "And, of course, I'll pray for you, too."

"Thank you, Coraline."

She turned to go, then stopped and looked over her shoulder. "And one more thing, Sam."

He looked at her.

"Look to your heart to guide you and you will never go wrong." With a knowing smile, she left the room.

And Sam was more confused than ever.

Chapter Sixteen

"So what did you want to talk about, son? Your call sounded urgent."

Sam looked at his dad across the table they were sitting at, next to the front window inside the Cozy Cup Café. "I'm dealing with a problem, and I need your advice."

"Okay, what's up?" His dad was as steady as they came, and Sam had often relied on his levelheaded guidance in the past. And now… Well, now, with his head and heart at war over a certain lovely bookstore owner, and the latest development in his backup-job search, Sam needed impartial counsel more than ever.

"I got a solid job offer from a school district in Florida I contacted last month."

"Hey, that's great." His father took a sip of hot tea. "I know you've been worried about losing your job ever since Randall Manufacturing closed."

"Yeah, a job offer is great. Except…"

Dad leaned in, his brow crinkled. "Except what?"

"I'm sure, given the gossip circuit in Bygones, you've heard that I've been spending some time with Allison True." Having lived in Bygones his whole life, his father knew everybody in town.

His dad nodded and set his spoon down. "I'd heard rumblings about that."

"Yeah, well, the thing is, I might have feelings for her, and taking the job would mean leaving Bygones."

An imaginary light went on over his father's head. "Ah. And also leaving Allison," he supplied.

"Exactly. She has to stay for two years, per the arrangement with the SOS Committee." Just the idea of saying goodbye to

Bygones—and Allison—had a painful tear ripping through Sam's chest.

"So let me see if I understand what you're telling me." His dad, an engineer by trade, was very analytical and very good at framing things in a sensible way. "You're in love with Allison—"

"I never said I was in love with her," Sam interjected.

His father gave him a sideways look. "You said you had feelings, and you're stressing over what to do about the job offer because it would mean leaving her, so I just assumed you loved her."

Sam fiddled with a napkin. "I'm not sure how I feel about her."

"But I'm assuming you like her, are attracted to her?" he asked, piercing Sam with his brown eyes.

All Sam could do was nod.

Dad frowned. "So?"

Sam scratched his cheek but stayed quiet. Somehow, acknowledging his feelings for Allison verbally made them seem so much more difficult to refute.

"What's going on here, Sammy?" Dad studied him. "You say you have feelings for her," he said, making air quotes around the word *feelings*. "Yet you aren't willing to discuss what these feelings might be, even though you're in a tough spot deciding whether to accept a job offer in Florida because of her."

"Crazy, huh?"

"Well, let's try to make it less crazy. Talk to me, let me help." He leaned back in his chair. "That's why you called me, right?"

Sam chewed his cheek. "Right."

His father just stared at him expectantly, his head slightly tilted to one side.

With such a life-altering decision on the line, Sam guessed it was time to spill; he really needed an outside perspective, one he trusted. "I'm falling for her, Dad, and it scares me stupid."

His dad nodded knowingly. "Ah, there's the rub."

"That about sums it up." Sam let out a weighty breath. "This has been eating at me for a while. Ever since Allison and I reconnected."

"Yeah, I can see that it's really got you in a knot. What I'm not quite so clear on is why loving Allison has you running scared."

Sam scrunched up his face. "You really have to ask that question?"

"I just did."

"I haven't exactly had the best loving-female role models in my life."

"You mean...your mom?" Dad asked, his voice low yet devoid of tone.

"And Teresa." Sam tightened his hands around his coffee cup. "The only two women I've ever loved, and both of them cut out on me."

His father shook his head. "Oh, boy."

"My sentiments exactly."

"Not surprising, I guess," his dad replied. "You probably think all women leave."

"It's not rocket science," Sam said.

"So you're afraid to let yourself admit you love Allison because you're afraid you'll eventually get hurt."

"That about sums it up."

"Have you told Allison any of this?"

"Not exactly."

"What do you mean? Either you've told her or you haven't."

Trust his dad to methodically pick stuff apart. Maybe that was what Sam needed, though maybe not what he wanted. Seemed he was getting a lesson in handling dichotomous emotions. "I told her I liked her, but also that I'm not ready for any kind of relationship."

"What did she say?"

"She agreed with me. She doesn't want a relationship, either."

"Have you told her about the job offer?"

"Nope. I wanted to talk to you first," Sam said.

"So you appreciate my opinion?"

"Of course."

"Then here it is." His dad leaned in. "You should be communicating with Allison about this."

"Even if it means tipping my hand?"

"Even then," his father said. "If there's anything I wish I'd done differently with your mom, it's that I wish we'd talked more."

Sam sat up, his interest piqued.

His dad went on. "Instead, I clammed up when she started drifting away, and by the time I decided we needed to hash things out, she was already gone."

"I didn't know that." Sam chewed on the interesting parallel his father had brought up. Sam had known that Teresa was unhappy with living in Bygones and being a stay-at-home mom. But he hadn't confronted the problem until she strayed and it was too late.

"I'm not always big on sharing, especially with you kids," Dad said.

"Then keeping stuff inside must be genetic."

"Must be. So what's the worst thing that could happen if you tell Allison how you feel?"

"She won't return my feelings, or she'll say she does and then take off on down the line."

"Okay." His father steepled his hands in front of his face. "And what's the worst thing that can happen if you *don't* tell her how you feel?"

Sam's gut pitched. "I could lose her."

Dad pointed at him. "Precisely. So you have

to decide—do you want to possibly lose her by letting your fears dictate your actions, which would mean keeping your feelings to yourself, or do you want to up your chances of ending up with Allison?"

"I just know that I don't want to lose her," Sam uttered. "I can't imagine life without her." Except as lonely and devoid of happiness. Not exactly an appealing prospect.

"And I didn't want to lose your mom, but I did because I was too clueless and closed off to realize what I needed to do until it was way too late." His father's voice resonated with sorrow; muted by time, yes, but still unmistakable. "Don't make the same mistakes I did, son. You'll regret it if you do, and that's a terrible price to pay, believe me."

All Sam could do was nod.

"And as long as you value my opinion, I'm going to throw this out."

"I expect nothing less," Sam replied.

His dad skewered him with a pointed look. "From what I can tell, you're in love with her, Sam, and that's a gift from God."

A gift from God. Wow. That was big. Sam

forced himself to consider what his dad had said, and all at once something fragile broke free in Sam's chest, flooding him with warmth, which brought forth a steely resolve to take a risk. To fully embrace the truth. "I... think you're right." Even though he'd fought it, he saw now that he loved Allison with his whole heart, and he couldn't squander that. "I have to gut up and tell her, and, honestly, doing so makes my stomach churn."

"Have you prayed about this?"

"Yes."

"Well, I'd pray more and let God know you're on board with His plan."

"Good idea." Allison had helped reestablish his relationship with God. Sam saw now that he needed to lean on Him for support in tough times. This qualified.

"Excellent." His father grinned. "Glad I could help. I'll look forward to seeing Allison. She must have turned into one amazing woman."

"She has, Dad. She's kind, loving and smart, not to mention drop-dead gorgeous."

Sam smiled. "Really, she's the most wonderful woman I've ever met."

"Then hold on to her, no matter what," his dad said, a shadow in his eyes. "I only wish I'd done the same."

"I'll do my best," Sam said. "I promise."

Though even his best wouldn't guarantee a happy ending.

"Are Sam and the kids coming to the service?" Viv asked Allison.

From their pew near the altar, Allison threw a glance toward the back of the church. "I'm not sure."

"But you hope so, right?" Viv asked with a twinkle in her voice, echoing Allison's exact thought.

Allison settled in place, her eyes forward, her back ramrod straight. "It would be nice, yes." Wonderful, actually. She hadn't seen Sam lately, and she'd missed him a lot. She loved Sam, and she had to tell him.

Even though just the thought of laying her heart on the line made her hands sticky.

"Oh, come on," Viv said, bringing Allison back to their conversation.

From the corner of her eye, Allison saw Viv shake her head. There might have been an eye roll there, too. "You've got it bad for Coach Franklin, don't you?" Viv asked.

Allison let her back sag. Keeping her feelings under wraps was wearing on her. She needed an ear. Desperately. She looked at Viv. "Yep, I kinda do."

"You don't seem too happy about that."

"Sam doesn't want to fall in love."

Viv waved a hand. "Oh, pshaw. I've seen the way he looks at you."

Allison's anxiety eased a bit, but didn't completely dissipate. "Well, I'm going to talk to him about it today, if possible. If the twins are around, my confession may need to wait, though."

"Seems like you're pretty taken with Nicky and Rosie. They're adorable," Viv said.

"Yes, I love them, too." If things went right—*please, God, hear my prayer*—the twins, along with Sam, would be in her life forever.

"In that vein, I have some news," Viv said.

"You do?" Allison said eagerly. "Spill."

"Yes." Viv sucked in a large breath. "I'm pushing forward with a plan I've had in place for a while, and I'm going to adopt a baby."

"Oh, Viv." Allison squeezed her friend's arm. "That's wonderful."

"Thank you."

"Have you found a baby yet?"

Viv shook her head. "No, and it might be a while. But I'm willing to wait."

"I didn't know you wanted kids," Allison said. "What made you want to adopt a child?"

"I've always wanted to be a mother, and this seemed like a good time." Viv smiled. "And I'm not getting any younger."

"Are you planning on having a biological child someday, when you meet the right man?" In Allison's mind, Viv deserved a houseful of kids, just like the one Viv had been part of, as one of six siblings.

Biting her lip, Viv looked away.

"Oh, that sounded wrong." Allison wondered where her tact had gone. "Obviously, I know how easy it is to love any child, whether that child is your biological child or not. I was just thinking that you should have lots of kids in your life."

"It's fine," Viv said, an uneasy smile on her lips. "I understand why you ask. I'm just going to take things one step at a time and see how everything goes. I've always wanted lots of kids, so...hopefully this will work out."

Vivian's tone had Allison wondering if Viv was holding something back. But what? Viv was a romantic, an old-fashioned girl with a kind heart and quick mind, though she didn't have a boyfriend at the moment. Allison had always thought Viv would make a wonderful mother.

Before Allison could formulate a reply, Viv's eyes went up and she gazed over Allison's shoulder. "Look who just rolled into church," Viv said, sotto voce, leaning in. "The man of the hour."

Allison's heart skittered. She turned just in time to see Sam sliding into their pew.

"Hey, you," he said, unbuttoning his charcoal-gray suit coat.

"You decided to come," Allison said, feeling a tad unbalanced. On the one hand, she was ecstatic to see him because she loved being with him. That was a given. On the other hand, now he was here, and she had to go through with telling him she loved him. Talk about the good, the bad and the hopefully not ugly.

"I did," he said. "The kids wouldn't have it any other way." He looked right into her eyes and held her gaze for a few long seconds.

She just about quit breathing.

"And neither would I," he added, giving her hand a squeeze.

Any reply was cut off by the church organ signaling the start of the service. Good thing. Allison wasn't sure she could form words just then.

But sooner or later she'd have to talk to Sam. And who knew how *that* conversation would turn out.

Hopefully not with any broken hearts.

After the church service ended, Sam and Allison went to the Sunday school classroom to collect Rosie and Nicky. As they did so,

Sam commended himself on keeping calm, cool and collected for the past hour, even with his plans for after the service looming.

As they headed back to the front of the church, Allison chatted happily with the twins, and he looked her over, really liking the way her navy blue dress contrasted with her brown hair and blue eyes. She had her hair down with just a few strands pulled back to one side, and the style really showed off her pretty bone structure.

Sitting beside her during the service had been wonderful and, really, he felt so close to her when they worshipped together. Honestly, he couldn't imagine attending church without her in the future. Hopefully, he wouldn't have to, but no one ever knew how things were going to turn out.

Another loss would take him out at the knees.

They reached the foyer and he caught sight of his dad standing by the double front doors, which had been flung wide. "There's Grandpa, kids," he said, pointing right. "Let's go see him."

The kids ran to Sam's dad and gave hugs all around. When Sam and Allison caught up, Sam made the reintroductions; though his dad and Allison were acquainted, it had been years since they'd seen each other. His father enfolded Allison in a bear hug, exclaiming how good it was to see her again.

Sam got both of the kids' attention. "Listen, you two. Grandpa is going to take you home for some of his famous waffles. Isn't that great?"

Both kids jumped up and down. "Will Smokey be there?" Nicky asked his grandpa. Smokey was his dad's black Lab, and the kids adored him.

"Of course," Sam's father said. "He's setting the table now."

"Dogs can't set tables," Rosie said.

"Well, Smokey is pretty smart, so why don't we go to my house and see how he did?"

His father said goodbye and then herded the kids outside. He lived only a few blocks away from the church, so Sam was sure they'd be walking to their grandpa's house. The sun was out, even though the temperature had dropped a bit as October had worn on.

Allison gave him a wary look. "Um… what's up?"

"What do you mean?"

"You just got rid of the kids."

"So I did." He gestured outside. "It's a nice day, and I thought you might want to go for a walk."

She inclined her head. "All right, sounds like a plan."

He offered her his arm. "Let's go."

Soon they were walking away from the church. Sam was intensely aware of Allison's hand grasping his upper arm. He suddenly wished he'd loosened his tie before they'd set off. It was really warming up out here. Of course, he always felt warm when Allison was around.

"Where are we going?" she asked.

"I thought it might be nice to just walk around and see the fall colors." He wanted privacy, and as soon as they got away from the church, things should be quiet.

"Excellent idea," she replied. "The leaves have really started turning lately."

They walked in silence for a while, and Sam simply let himself enjoy being with Allison. He tried to ignore the anxiety poking holes in his confidence, but there was just no way to get around the fact that he was going out on a limb here.

He needed to lay his heart on the line like never before. For him. And Allison. He liked the sound of their names together.

Soon they reached Granary Road. He guided her right, away from town. As they walked, silence descended, and the only sound he heard was the rustling of the wind in the red, gold and yellow leaves on the trees next to the road.

"Sam—"

"Allison," he said at exactly the same time.

He paused. So did she.

He gestured to her. "You first."

"I'm assuming you have something you want to talk about." She read him well. But then, she was very intuitive, just one of the many things he loved about her.

"Actually, I do."

"Go on," she said softly, stopping under a large oak tree that stood between two Victorian houses on large lots. "I'm listening." She adjusted herself so she was facing him more squarely. Her eyes were the same color of the blue, blue sky at her back. Stunning.

He cleared his throat and resisted the urge to touch her silky hair. *Focus, Franklin.* "Well, the thing is, I've been offered a job with a school district in Florida."

For the barest second she froze, her face suspended in a completely blank expression. She blinked once, very slowly, and then, as if she'd flicked on a switch, she smiled mechanically and exclaimed, "Hey! That's great."

Her response took him aback. He gulped. "It is?"

"Oh, yes, it's fantastic news." She patted his hand impersonally, kind of like she was petting a dog, and gave him another odd smile devoid of true warmth. "This is what you wanted, right?"

"Well, yes, I guess it is." Until he'd met her. And then everything had changed. But it was looking as if she didn't feel the same way. If she did, wouldn't she be distressed by this news? Not that he wanted her to be upset—

"Then it's fantastic," she added, shifting away from him, back a few steps. Instantly, it was as if she'd put up an invisible, foot-thick wall.

He felt the distance keenly, and wanted more than anything to pull her into his arms and never let her go. "I'm…" *Devastated.* "Not sure what to say."

"I think you've said everything necessary."

Man, she sounded impersonal. He hated it, hated the chasm that had opened up between them the minute he'd told her about the job offer. "I want to know what you think about the move," he asked to keep the conversation going. Anything was better than letting things go now.

"This is what's best for your family, right?" she asked, looking, he was certain, over his shoulder rather than at him, as if she was trying to keep herself from connecting visually. Or in any way, really. Something shriveled inside him.

"Maybe," he said in a noncommittal way, floundering.

"I mean, you have to have a job, right?" she said offhandedly, as if she was discussing the weather.

"Right." The word felt bitter on his tongue. He already had a job that he liked and wanted to keep. But that was out of his control.

"Then moving to Florida is what's best." Her voice had become uncharacteristically monotone, and it grated like sandpaper on his heart.

He fisted his hands. This was wrong, just standing here, watching her slip away. He said the first thing that occurred to him. "Will you even miss us?" he asked, trying to keep his voice even and failing. Because he'd sure miss her. His heart clenched.

"Of course," she said. "But I'll be really busy at work and with the creative-writing group, so I'll be fine."

He frowned. "That's it?"

"I guess so," she replied brightly. He'd never seen her like this, so…impersonal. So distant. This wasn't Allison. A numb sense of loss froze up his insides and suddenly his hopes for love washed away, leaving him empty and hollow, as if someone had filled him with ice cubes.

He'd lost her. Had he ever really had her, though?

"Was there anything else you wanted to talk about?" she asked stiffly. "I...have to get to work."

Work. What mattered to her. Not him. Happy Endings. He shouldn't be surprised; she'd made it clear what her priorities were. He'd been an idiot to think she'd ever love him. "No, I think we've covered all the pertinent details."

"Okay, then. Bye, Sam." She blinked several times. "Um...I think I'll just...keep walking this way for a while, if you don't mind."

He couldn't even speak, could barely stand upright. As he turned to walk away and she went the opposite direction, he let his shoulders sag. Allison didn't love him. He'd lost her. And all he had to show for it was a broken heart and a job he didn't want waiting for him in Florida.

Allison walked away from Sam. Tears burned her eyes, with panic building inside her so quickly she could barely think, much less speak.

Fool. Fool. Fool. She'd known she shouldn't have let Sam under her skin, into her heart, into her very soul. This pain was what she'd wanted to avoid, what she'd been so afraid of.

She'd meant to tell him she loved him— oh, she had!—until he'd thrown her a curve with the job offer. But now, would it be right to tell him she loved him if it might throw a wrench into his plans? She wanted what was best for him and the kids. Who was she to take that away from him by flinging her feelings at him?

But…she loved him, and Nicky and Rosie. With everything in her. Could she really keep that to herself? Could she really let him walk away without telling him the truth?

Her love had turned into a double-edged

sword, capable of cutting her from both directions.

What do I do, Lord?

She heard Sam's footsteps pause. She stopped, too. Soon he'd be miles away, and so would the twins. A profound sense of loss roared through her and it felt as if she'd been kicked in the ribs.

She pressed a shaking hand to her chest, holding back a sob. No, she couldn't walk away. She had to tell him, she couldn't second-guess him, not about something so important. So life changing. She'd kept her feelings for him secret once before, and she regretted that. There would be no more regrets.

She wiped her damp cheeks, and then spun around. "Sam, wait."

From thirty feet away, he turned. "Yes?"

"I…I have to tell you something."

He hesitated. "And…I have to tell you something."

A good thing or a bad thing? She drew in a shaky breath. Either way, she had to level with him or she'd never know what might have been. With determination she raised a hand and gestured toward herself, trying to ignore her trembling knees. "Come here."

He walked slowly back, and then, just about the time she wanted to scream at him to go faster, he stood before her, his brown eyes gazing right into hers.

"I...well...I haven't been completely honest with you," she said, bowing her head. "See, the thing is, there's a reason I told you I was happy for you about the job offer." She opened her mouth to tell him she loved him.

He silenced her with a finger pressed to her lips. "Shh." He put his hands on her shoulders and squeezed. Warmth spread downward. "First, before you talk, I need to tell you why I was upset by your reaction to my news."

"Okay," she whispered.

"I've been so afraid to tell you the truth. But I'm through letting my fear call the shots. I love you, Allison True," he declared, cupping her jaw. "And as long as you're here in Bygones, this is where I want to be." Allison hesitated, her blue gaze fixed on him, her lips trembling and her eyes wide.

And all at once, Sam felt the constraints of his past unwind from his heart. He took her soft, small hands in his. "My dad told me not to make the same mistakes he did with my mom, that I would regret it if I did, and that that would be a terrible price to pay."

"Go on," Allison told him, her hands shaking in his.

"From there, I realized the twins deserved a father who would do everything in his power to keep a woman like you in all our lives." He drew in a rough breath. "Think how different my life would have been if my dad had been more open with my mom."

"Oh, Sam," Allison said, tears welling in her eyes. "You're braver than I am."

"No, I'm not. I had to take this leap." He touched her cheek, loving its velvety smoothness. "No matter what happens, you're worth the risk, and I'll know that I did everything possible to keep you in my life."

Allison stared at him for a few agonizing moments, tears brimming and running down her cheeks. "You are the most amazing man I've ever met, and I adore your kids."

He waited, his heart thudding harder than it ever had.

She touched his cheek with trembling fingers. "I love you, too," she said, her voice breaking. "With all my heart."

Relief and happiness and joy slammed through him. He hugged her hard, burying his nose in her peach-scented hair. "I can't tell you how happy that makes me."

She pulled back and touched his cheek. "Try."

"This happy," he said, bending his head and kissing her.

She kissed him back, and everything was right in his world. After a while, he nibbled his way to her ear and said, "Were you really okay with us moving to Florida?"

"I was trying to be."

He settled back a bit, but kept his arms around her. "Why?"

She wiped moisture away from her face. "Because I love you enough to let you go and do what you have to for your family."

Her love humbled him. Completed him. *Thank You, God.*

He kissed her forehead. "So you were trying to be unselfish?"

"Yes. I knew I loved you, and I didn't want to lose you, but I wanted you and Nicky and Rosie to be happy and fulfilled most of all."

"You didn't want to stand in my way." She was truly one of the most giving, unselfish people he'd ever known. How had he ended up with someone so perfect?

She nodded. "It was a sacrifice I was willing to make."

Warmth and peace moved through him in a healing tide. "You're what's best for us," he said. "For now and always."

"I see that now." She smiled shakily. "But note the word *try.* I'm not sure I'm going to be able to keep myself away for long. I'm going to visit you guys as often as I can."

Once again, she amazed him. Whether he was here in Bygones or there in Florida, she'd love him and stand by him.

Suddenly, another decision was made easy. "About that. I'm going to turn down the job in Florida. It's too soon to take it, really. If I lose my job here—which I don't think I will because you and the other SOS shopkeepers are doing a great job and things are on the right track—then I'll start looking. Until then, I'm staying put, here with you."

"Are you sure? Because we could do long distance for the foreseeable future."

"You'd do that?"

"For you and the twins? Yes. Anything."

Again, this woman humbled him. "Well, I don't want to be away from you at all, so I'm staying. We'll cross the job bridge when we need to, together, but not before."

"Good." She looked at him from under her lashes. "I like the way you think."

"And I like how you always seem to have our best interests at heart," he said, again awed by her love and willingness to put him and the twins ahead of everything else.

"I love you, and the kids, so you're going to have to get used to me wanting good things for you guys."

"I think I can find a way to adjust to that," he said, pulling her closer.

"Good. I'm glad." She kissed him tenderly and laid a soft hand on his cheek. "So it looks like we have a perfect ending to our own storybook romance, don't we?"

"We sure do." He grinned against her lips as a profound sense of contentment and bliss bubbled through him. "Too bad I didn't realize I should have been with you all along."

"I'm glad you finally figured it out."

"I know a good thing when I see it." Though it had taken him many years to get smart. "Better late than never."

"You've got that right, Mr. Franklin," she said, moving closer, her gaze on his lips, her eyes soft with love. For him.

That look did him in. Without waiting another second he kissed her right, slowly and deeply, with all the love in his heart, with everything he had.

A car horn sounded. He broke away and looked over his shoulder, his arms still around Allison. Coraline's well-kept blue sedan rolled to a stop next to the curb. Coraline was driving, and Miss Mars, who always rode to and from church with Coraline, sat in the passenger seat.

Coraline rolled down her window and regarded them with a smile. "So it looks like the two of you have worked things out."

Allison's arms tightened around him. "You could say that."

Miss Mars leaned over. "Goo-goo eyes all over again."

"And heart," Sam said.

"Yes, I definitely have a goo-goo heart," Allison said.

"Wonderful," Coraline said. "God is good."

"Yes, He is," Sam said.

"Would you like a ride back into town?" Coraline asked.

"No," Sam said. "It's only a few blocks."

"You two probably want some alone time, don't you?" Miss Mars said, nodding her head so vigorously the small blue hat she wore bobbed down onto her forehead.

Allison smiled up at him. "Yes, I think we do," she said.

"All right, then," Coraline said, smiling

brightly. "Carry on." With that, she drove slowly away.

"Coraline had it right all along," Sam said.

"Yes, she did." Allison moved her hands to his shoulders. "I only wish I'd realized that sooner."

"Me, too," he replied. "We have a lot of kissing to catch up on."

"You read my mind," Allison said. And then she pulled him down for a long, sweet kiss that made his toes tingle and his heart perfectly complete.

And that would be all he and the twins would ever need.

* * * * *

Dear Reader,

I hope you enjoyed book four in THE HEART OF MAIN STREET continuity series. Bygones was a wonderful setting for a love story, and I enjoyed writing about Sam and Allison and how they found faith and love in the most unexpected yet wonderful way. Love isn't always easy or obvious, and it is gratifying to write stories that bring two people together through their mutual faith, shared values and love for the Lord, despite conflicts along the way. I think this story shows that if we trust in God's plan, we will always find love.

I want to thank my fellow Love Inspired authors Arlene James, Carolyne Aarsen, Brenda Minton, Charlotte Carter and Valerie Hansen. I loved working with these talented ladies, and as the newbie on the block, I learned so much from all of them. I hope we get the chance to work together again.

Please be sure to look for the next two installments of THE HEART OF MAIN STREET in the next two months.

May God bless you always.

Lissa Manley

Questions for Discussion

1. Have you read any of other books in THE HEART OF MAIN STREET continuity series? If so, how did this story connect to the others? Did the other books make you want to keep reading the series? Which was your favorite book so far? What did you like about it?

2. Allison loved Sam from afar in high school but never told anyone, not even her best friend, Lori. Discuss how you have kept something to yourself in the past, and whether or not you wished later you had shared it with another person.

3. Lori discouraged Sam from asking Allison out in high school. Was this justified, and if not, what might have been a better way for her to react? In your opinion, was she selfish, or merely trying to protect Allison?

4. Sam took his lawyer's advice and didn't date in case his ex-wife might use a ro-

mantic relationship against him in a custody battle. Was he weak for giving in, or was he just being a good father? What might have been some of his other options? Should he have called Teresa out on this? Discuss.

5. Do you think Sam was using the custody issue as the wrong way to keep his heart safe? Why or why not?

6. What was your favorite scene in the book and why? Who was your favorite character? Discuss.

7. Discuss how Nicky and Rosie served to bring Allison and Sam together, and how and why children can bridge the gaps in relationships.

8. Allison wanted to prove to herself, and her parents, that she could run Happy Endings. Have you ever felt the need to do this in your life? Were you successful?

9. Sam continued to see Allison because the kids loved being with her. Discuss why

you do or do not think he was using this as an excuse to see Allison. Was he being honest with himself?

10. Was Allison too ambitious, too hung up on making Happy Endings a success? Why or why not? Did her ambition make sense given her parents' doubts?

11. Were Allison and Sam believable characters? What did you like or dislike about each? Did the romance build believably?

12. Sam doubted his skills as a single father. Was this justified, given Teresa's opinion of him? Should he have been more confident? Or was he simply struggling with a difficult situation?

13. The bible verse in the beginning of the book was: "I can do all things in Him who strengthens me." Discuss the meaning of this verse and how it relates to the book.

14. Allison's mom and dad neglected their daughters for work. Given their background, was this understandable? Was

Allison's mom's turnaround believable? Discuss how someone's life experiences can affect their lives down the road.

15. Allison was going to walk away from Sam and let him go to Florida because she wanted what was best for him and the kids. But then she realized she loved them too much to walk away. Discuss whether you think her first reaction was reasonable, and whether she did the right thing by stopping him.

REQUEST YOUR FREE BOOKS!

2 FREE RIVETING INSPIRATIONAL NOVELS IN TRUE LARGE PRINT PLUS 2 FREE MYSTERY GIFTS

YES! Please send me 2 FREE Love Inspired® Suspense True Large Print novels and my 2 FREE mystery gifts (gifts are worth about $10). After receiving them, if I don't wish to receive any more books, I can return the shipping statement marked "cancel." If I don't cancel, I will receive 3 brand-new true large print novels every month and be billed just $7.99 per book in the U.S. or $9.99 per book in Canada. That's a savings of at least 20% off the cover price. It's quite a bargain! Shipping and handling is just 50¢ per book in the U.S. and 75¢ per book in Canada.* I understand that accepting the 2 free books and gifts places me under no obligation to buy anything. I can always return the shipment and cancel at any time. Even if I never buy another book, the two free books and gifts are mine to keep forever.

124/324 IDN F5GD

Name	(PLEASE PRINT)

Address	Apt. #

City	State/Prov.	Zip/Postal Code

Signature (if under 18, a parent or guardian must sign)

Mail to the **Harlequin® Reader Service:**
IN U.S.A.: P.O. Box 1867, Buffalo, NY 14240-1867
IN CANADA: P.O. Box 609, Fort Erie, Ontario L2A 5X3

* Terms and prices subject to change without notice. Prices do not include applicable taxes. Sales tax applicable in N.Y. Canadian residents will be charged applicable taxes. Offer not valid in Quebec. This offer is limited to one order per household. Not valid for current subscribers to Love Inspired Suspense True Large Print books. All orders subject to credit approval. Credit or debit balances in a customer's account(s) may be offset by any other outstanding balance owed by or to the customer. Please allow 4 to 6 weeks for delivery. Offer available while quantities last.

Your Privacy—The Harlequin® Reader Service is committed to protecting your privacy. Our Privacy Policy is available online at www.ReaderService.com or upon request from the Harlequin Reader Service.

We make a portion of our mailing list available to reputable third parties that offer products we believe may interest you. If you prefer that we not exchange your name with third parties, or if you wish to clarify or modify your communication preferences, please visit us at www.ReaderService.com/consumerschoice or write to us at Harlequin Reader Service Preference Service, P.O. Box 9062, Buffalo, NY 14269. Include your complete name and address.